Dancing Partners

BILL PEARSON

BOOK DOMAIN LLC
Publish to Perfection

Book Domain LLC.
543 E Louise Dr Phoenix, Az 85050

Ordering Information:

Amount Deals. Special rebates are accessible on the amount bought by corpora-tions, associations, and others. For points of interest, contact the distributor at the address above.

Printed in the United States of America.

ISBN-13   Paperback   978-1-970309-17-1
          eBook   978-1-970309-16-4

Contents

Prologue

The Old Groaner at the starting gate

ON THE MORNING OF 14 September, 1970, Bing Crosby arrived alone at the Del Mar racetrack, parked his car and walked to his private box to join a few friends, who were already in their seats, expecting his arrival.

Crosby had been the prime force in the development of the track in 1936, the principal stockholder for the first few years, and felt as at home there as anywhere. He was seldom bothered by fans in this setting, and as unconcerned about his personal security as any ordinary citizen.

He didn't notice the man who saw him walk from the parking lot, and followed him, increasing his own pace until he was only a few yards behind the aging star.

The ever affable Bing greeted the men in his box with a cheery hello. One of them was the mayor of San Diego, one of them, on a rare day off, the feisty jockey Willie Shoemaker, who only the week before had won a race riding a filly named Dares J to surpass John Longden as the most winning rider of all time. Willie had brought along a new friend, a young boxer with a lot of potential, but whose license had been suspended…

Just as Crosby opened the little gate to enter the box, the man closing in behind him brought something shiny and sharp out of his pocket, and with his other hand reached for Bing's shoulder. Shoemaker, acting instinctively, jumped out of his seat and punched the intruder in the chest with both open hands, sending him tumbling back to the aisle and down several steps.

There was a short scuffle, but it turned out the man was simply holding a silver pen that glinted in the sun, and all he wanted was an autograph.

It was over in a few minutes, and the rest of the day went as planned. The incident didn't even make the papers or the local TV news that evening.

Chapter 1

From New York to London in a flash

ON THAT SAME DAY A man named Robert Trabur boarded a plane at New York's Laguardia airport for an international flight direct, with only one stopover in Los Angeles, to London, England. He was dressed in a suit but was otherwise dubiously distinctive. 30 years old, 5'10" tall, about 165 pounds, wearing glasses, he might have been anything. A salesman, an athlete, a drug dealer, a minister, a spy, anything at all. Nobody else on the flight cared, one way or the other. They were involved in their own lives.

A good deal of Trabur's time during the long trip, trapped in his seat, was spent fantasizing about a certain Miss Debra Lavish, the love of his life. Not the usual carnal fantasies of the common man, but rather lofty ethereal projections of his feminine ideal, perched decoratively on a golden throne, the object of every man's desire. With his help, she was destined for stardom, of that he was certain.

The rest of his time was filled by apprehensively anticipating his business in London, and his sole contact there. The dealings might be more precarious than the initial preparations indicated, the outcome uncertain even if everything went smoothly. He couldn't sleep at all until the plane was well over the Atlantic, the engines a steady drone, and nothing but blackness beyond the windows.

Chapter 2

An old ham, desperate in Soho

THE MAN IN THE SHADOWS wasn't a habitual mugger, but it was a damp, murky night in Soho, and he didn't have enough to pay for a cot, so it was either walk the streets until dawn and then hope to catch a nap on a park bench without being bothered by a passing bobby… or knock over one of the swells who came staggering out of a pub after having one too many.

All he needed was a pound or two. Tomorrow would be a full day of new opportunities for the inveterate optimist. He'd been at the top long enough to believe he belonged there, but since then he'd been on the margin, and now he'd hit rock bottom after a nasty lurch of fate. He'd been handsome once, a man of pride and accomplishment. Now he was ugly in his desperation.

It seemed like it was always foggy in Soho, even when the moon shone brightly over the rest of London. The narrow cobblestone streets, the gray walls of the unkempt slum tenements, the dimlit pubs on every corner, it all turned the world into a menacing maze of misery, every step a gamble, every corner a hazard.

And there he was, not off his footing, but with a mincing gait, a chubby well-dressed fellow who looked like an easy mark. There was no one else in sight, as the man in the shadows rushed up behind him. Hearing his approach, the toff turned, and they both recognized the other!

For a moment Gordon Feastwell cringed, stepping back in a defensive posture to fully face the equally startled stalker. "Sonnie! What are you—"

"Oh, I'm sorry…" he retreated as well, "I… I saw you, and wanted to call out, but… It's been so long… I've forgotten your name."

They stood there in the darkness, each readjusting their perspective on this sudden encounter. Feastwell was certain he'd narrowly avoided an attack, and didn't know quite how to react.

"It's been years, Sonnie… years." He didn't feel at all like spending another moment with this apparition out of his past, but it seemed the only thing to do with the desolate looking fellow.

"Let's pop in here," he indicated the sign in front of a cellar pub just up the alley. "We'll have a pint and catch up."

There were only a few grizzled regulars in the place as they found their way to a table and sat down to stare across and take stock of each other.

"I saw you earlier this evening, that's why I recalled your name right away," Feastwell admitted. "I was down here in this neighborhood to check out a young comedian… but he was right green. I saw you, but by the time I fully remembered who you were, you'd passed by."

After taking his first swallow of beer, Sonnie felt a fresh flush of enthusiasm. From the brink of a desperate criminal act, he'd been switched back to civility in one blinking second.

"How's thee dad, then?" he asked. Feastwell's father had been Sonnie's agent years earlier, his son then an assistant, learning the business.

"He's been gone ten years, Sonnie. Where have you been…?"

"Here and there and back again. In Brighton mostly. I had a job."

"In the business?"

"No. Just a job. The place closed down. I won't kid you, Feastwell, I'm tapped out. Any chance you could loan me a few bob…?"

"Cor blimey, lad. To be sure."

Pulling out his wallet, the man found two pounds, and passed them across the table.

"I'm not carrying much tonight." There was no need to explain why.

"I'll pay thee back…"

"Ech, by gum. Put away. Listen, you should come up to me office tomorrow. I might be able to get you a few bits. Can't promise anything, though."

After finishing their drinks and exiting the pub, the two men shook hands and Feastwell watched the shabby ghost of a former acquaintance disappear back into the shadows. He took a deep breath of the foul night air, realizing full well their reunion might have turned out very differently.

Chapter 3

So this is England

ARRIVING AT HEATHROW AT THE edge of London, Trabur took a cab directly to the Europa hotel, where a reservation had been secured. The driver accompanied him to the lobby, knowing he'd not have English money to pay the fare, and the clerk took care of it as Trabur registered and turned over several traveler's checks for safe keeping in the hotel safe. A crisply uniformed bellboy grabbed his bags and showed him the way up the elevator to his room, graciously accepting the two American dollars offered for the service. Whoever he was, he obviously had an expense account. Making sure there was a 'do not disturb' notice posted outside the door before locking it, Trabur made a quick telephone call from his room, then went straight to bed where he remained for a solid five and about three syrupy hours.

Chapter 4

A photographer, playing at work

Photographer Lance Rainer and his assistant Betty were going over their assignments for the next week. As only one of two staff photographers for Sears, Lance was responsible for all the company's newspaper and magazine ads, the color photos of beautiful people wearing the clothes Sears hoped to sell to all the less beautiful people who shopped in their stores.

It wasn't the most fulfilling job a good photographer might aspire to, but then again, it was better than being the one who took all of Sears' products photographs, a far less interesting occupation.

"Let's call Alice and… Pat for sure, for dresses, Monday." He was trying to recall the names of a couple of his favorite models.

"What about Tuesday… coats and accessories?"

"I don't know," he thought about it, "None of the girls like coats, especially this time of year." Summer was hanging on with record temperatures for September.

"What about Debra?" Betty suggested.

"Oh, miss attitude…. She'd be alright, if it's not her time of the month."

"We all have to put with that, Lance," she protested.

"I know, but Debra seems unable to conceal her moods. Remember when we tried some lingerie shots with her?"

"I remember."

"Her body was okay, but she was giving me seductive expressions, and I couldn't get her to damp it down and put out the aloof pan those shots call for."

"She's not very experienced," Betty tried to make a reasonable excuse, but didn't press it. She never played favorites.

"No more bra and panties layouts with Debra." His verdict was final.

"I'll make a note," Betty replied, making a brief entry in her notebook.

"We'll need just about everybody in the rolodex next week."

"Okay, I'll alert them all, and set up a tentative schedule."

"Give me a little more time between set-ups than you have been lately. You've had me racing through the days."

"Just trying to make sure we make all the deadlines, boss."

"Uh huh," he sighed, "I need a week in Barbados. Schedule that. Will you."

"Oh sure. Doesn't matter to me."

Chapter 5

A girl with grit and a guy with gumption

CASSANDRA THIMBLE AND SHLUG MUGGER, along with two more of their stable mates, only had the exclusive use of the Newcastle racecourse for two hours, but even then there was no restriction on anyone who wanted to hang around or sit in the bleachers to watch whatever was happening.

It was Casey's turn to ride Big Winston, give him a serious workout and find out how fast he could run. The owner had hopes he could enter the stallion in that season's upcoming races. Dressed in regulation breeches and boots, Casey easily mounted the nervous steed.

Shlug heard "Nice haunches on that filly," from a layabout loitering just outside the rail, and his buddy's "I'll say," in agreement.

Since Big Winston obviously wasn't a filly, it was equally obvious whose haunches the blokes were admiring.

He turned and took a few purposeful steps toward the men, until he was well within their discomfort zone. He was a few inches shorter than either of them, but it wasn't a factor in the matter.

"Have you got any business here, laddies?" Shlug asked gruffly.

One fellow took a step back, the other inched sideways, "Not really."

"Well, I have," Shlug declared, "so bugger off!"

There was no mistaking his message, or their response. The two loafers backed away and shuffled down the track toward the exit, followed every step of the way by Shlung's steely stare.

Casey wasn't aware of any disturbance, concentrating on wheeling Big Winston around, in place, in preparation for a serious, all out gallop around the track.

Casey and Shlug were an improbable pair, the way she would have thought about it if she ever did think about it, which she didn't, but Shlug had a few indistinct ideas of his own. He was three years older and three inches shorter than she was, but Shlug had loved Casey since they were children together, both in love with the magnificent horses in her grandfather's stable. Well, maybe love was too strong a word for their relationship. She thought of Shlug as a brother, and he thought of her as a cousin with sex appeal. She was the trainer and he was the ranch jockey, too husky now to compete as a professional but very valuable in the complex training that every racehorse must undergo.

They both took their orders from her grandfather, Mortimer Poundstack, the lord of the castle and everything attached to it. Born Cassandra, she'd insisted on being called Casey ever since she could remember, hating the sissy name she'd been christened. She didn't care for any of the delicate habits of most young ladies her age, preferring the tomboy personality she'd acquired around the stables, mixing with the mostly rowdy males who populated the racing world she knew and thrived in as well as any of them.

Shlug kept his distance, and his own counsel, not even hinting to his pals that he adored the mule-headed maid of the manor. Only her father, his one true friend, long absent from the British Isles, Dingle Thimble himself, knew anything about Shlug's dear devotion, and had sworn over a bottle of certified hundred year old whiskey never to tell.

When it looked like Big Winston was settled enough to start, and Shlug had set his stopwatch, he shouted "Go!" and Casey dug her heels into the horse's sides with the practiced precise sharpness to put him in motion.

It was a sure start, and smooth acceleration until he was too far away for a good view of his stride, but he seemed to be moving along at a very respectable speed.

Casey brought him back through the starting point at full gallop, not letting the horse relax and slow to a trot until well past.

Shlug frowned at the time he'd noted on a card to be delivered to Poundstack later.

Casey stayed in the saddle, and walked the horse all around the track before dismounting and unsaddling the beast. The lads took him to the truck, as Casey joined Shlug.

"How'd he do?" she asked her staunch pal, already knowing it couldn't have been very outstanding by his sober attitude.

"No improvement since we last clocked him," he sighed, "in fact, a few seconds slower."

"I don't think Big Winston is going to be a champion racer," Casey's verdict unnecessary to Shlug. Even with a rider weighing fifteen pounds less than either of them, Poundstack's best horse of the year didn't have a chance in any professional race, and they both knew it.

Chapter 6

Devious developments in London

ROBERT TRABUR MADE ONE VERY important long distance call, early on the first morning of his visit to London, enjoyed what his waiter called a traditional English breakfast in the hotel dining room, then proceeded to walk leisurely for over an hour on a seemingly haphazard route along Grosvenor Square, which surrounded the hotel. Finally he hailed a cab, which took him a few miles outside the center of the city to a residential row of well maintained townhouses. There was a brief argument with the driver because he had still neglected to exchange dollars for pounds, but it ended amicably when the cabman realized he would end up with a substantial tip when he made the exchange himself.

Without hesitation for more than a few seconds to acclimate himself to his surroundings, Trabur made his way to the entrance of a particular house, and rang the bell.

A cheerful older man, Lywellen Fister, opened the door within seconds, obviously waiting expectantly for his visitor, and delighted to see him. Fister was overweight and overwrought, it seemed to Trabur, speaking rapidly and with little forethought. In contrast, his guest spoke sparsely while they got acquainted, situated themselves comfortably around Fister's large dining room table and each held a hot cup of tea in his hand.

"I'm so pleased your firm will be publishing my book, Mr. Trabur. I'm most certain it will be of interest in your country as well as mine."

"Our publisher and editors believe it will, Mr. Fister."

Not a salesman, an athlete, a drug dealer, a minister or a spy, Trabur was merely a humble book editor. Specializing in popular culture, and the one on staff most familiar with show business history, he had been designated to make the trip, interview this retired publicity man, and select the book's contents from the fellow's vast collection of photos he'd accumulated over a half century. It was a task he anticipated eagerly, looking forward as well to as many or more pleasant hours exploring the English capital and surrounding countryside over the next couple of weeks. This was his first excursion outside the borders of the USA.

The air in Fister's home seemed foul, and Trabur couldn't ignore it. When the man pulled out a cigar and put a match to it, his visitor made a request.

"Would you mind opening a window if you're going to smoke? I'm not a smoker myself, and it's—"

"Oh, of course," Fister replied, and jumped to the window in a couple of bouncing hops. He opened the window wide, and there was an immediate rush of fresh air from outside.

So Fister smoked, and Trabur moved his chair closer to the window, and their relationship proceeded in this manner, professionally, and with diplomacy employed by both men, Trabur trying to adjust to the annoying habits of his host, and Fister willing to make any adjustments required to maintain the good will of the Galactic Publishing Company of New York, London and Paris, the respected old firm interested in publishing his illustrated history of British show business of the first half of the 20th century.

A proposal had been made, officially, in a document of several pages, and a tentative publishing date had been set, but a final contract would not be signed by either party until Trabur had finished his work. For the first time, after five years at the company, he was authorized to sign for the company if he decided the material warranted publication.

Both were anxious to proceed to the job at hand.

"I assume the first thing you should see is the material I've selected for the English edition." Fister suggested, and he was already pulling out large folders from a deep shelved object of furniture against the wall which appeared to be an antique itself. Spreading it out to fill the dining room table, the material was well organized, with title chapters for the book on top of various sized mounds of old photos, posters and pressbooks.

"Ah," sighed Trabur, estimating several hours perusing it all, fifty years of people and productions, most of which he knew nothing of and couldn't care less about. And all to be accompanied by Fister's thickly accented narration.

Taking out a notebook and pen from his briefcase, Trabur, without realizing he was doing it, sighed again, "Ah…"

Finally, after it seemed at least half of eternity had passed, the individual piles were neatly stacked into one which rose to an imposing height, his notebook was full of shorthand reminders to himself, and Trabur had a detailed concept of Fister's proposed book.

"What do you think?" the old conniver asked, timidly. He was confident he had a tremendous book, but he'd spent his life promoting talented people others often considered without value, so he also knew about rejection.

"If the English are as enamored of movie stars as Americans are, this will be a best seller."

"I *knew* you'd think so," Fister burbled, almost beside himself.

One of him was quite enough for Trabur, however, so he brought him back to sobriety with a serious caveat, "I'm not sure about an American edition though."

"Oh, you've only seen a fraction of my collection! I have hundreds of photos of American performers... *rare* photos, never printed in the states, when they were working here in England!"

"I've seen enough for one day... more than enough. We've made a lot of progress. If it goes this smoothly, it shouldn't take more than a week to—"

"Whatever it takes, Mr. Trabur," Fister interrupted, "How about joining me for dinner? There's a nice restaurant not far from here..."

"Thank you, no," Trabur said with finality, without bothering to explain why not.

"In that case I'll just ring up a taxi," Fister said, ever accommodating.

Which is what he did.

Chapter 7

A princess-in-waiting in Queens

Debra Lavish was only half finished, painting her nails, when the phone rang. She picked up the receiver carefully, trying to keep from scraping her wet fingertips.

"Hello, this is Debra," she cooed.

"Hello Debra, this is Betty, with Sears."

"Hi Betty."

"How's your schedule for next Tuesday?"

"Let's see…" She didn't have a thing pending any day next week, "I think I'm free Tuesday."

"Good. We can give you four hours Tuesday. Coats and accessories."

"Coats and accessories?" Debra could just imagine herself being lost behind piles of fur and leather. "When are you going to shoot me in dresses?"

"You'll get your chance in every category in time. Lance has a long list of models, you know."

"Okay. Coats and accessories."

"Don't fret, girl. There will probably be a couple of cute hats, and that calls for closeups. You'll probably end up with a few shots for your portfolio."

"What time Tuesday?"

"Make it 10 AM. Don't be late."

"I'll see you then."

"Do you remember how to get here?"

"Same place, isn't it?"

"Same place. 50th and Park."

"Thanks, Betty."

She put back the phone cautiously, examined her nails, and went back to the job.

Catalog modeling was a bore, but it paid fairly well, and it could lead to more prestigious work, and then, well…

She stood up and examined her image in the dressing table mirror with a critical but ultimately approving eye, an exercise she performed far more often than was necessary. She was dressed only in a lacy bra and panties, not for anyone's admiring glances except her own, as she lounged about her apartment most days when she wasn't working or looking for work.

As for Tuesday, there'd be no chance of a show or even dinner that evening in the city. Her usual escort, reliable Robert, was away somewhere, and there wasn't anybody else she could tolerate for more than ten minutes. The world was full of handsome, exciting men, but where were they hiding? All she ever met were jerks like Chuck, the crude salesman on the first floor with a stupid mustache who kept asking her for a date every time they met at the pool… or Tony, the fat middle-aged Italian who owned the only nearby restaurant she felt comfortable dining in by herself… or that other photographer, who paid even less than Sears, and only wanted photos of her in vintage 1920's full body swimming costumes. What a freak that guy was! His pictures were worthless to her, and she only posed for him when she was nearly broke, needing rent money.

If Robert only had a bigger bankroll, and a more forceful personality, she might consider taking him on as a husband. It would be just as easy to make it as a movie star if married, and she'd have a secure base to work from. She didn't love him, she didn't even particularly like him, but he was so pliable, he'd play by her rules, which would be her first requirement for any prospective husband.

Ah, well. She made a slow turn and threw back her head to send her long golden hair around in a lovely swirl. What did any of those Hollywood bimbos like Lauren Hutton or Mamie Van Doren have that she didn't have? She was patient. Her time would come.

Chapter 8

Big surprise for a closet fan

THAT EVENING, AFTER HIS BUSY day with the accommodating but rather tiresome elderly Englishman, Trabur took in a bit of London's night life, as much as he figured his limited budget could stand without strain, and drank just a bit less than he could handle without passing out. Fortunately he was back in his room before that occurred, and by morning he was ready for another round with the formidable old publicity man.

It was almost noon before he arrived at Fister's residence. The cab made its way through foggy streets without a comment from the driver, as if it were a normal kind of day, so apparently it was. The day before, bright and sunny, might have been more unusual.

"You've got some great photos, alright," Trabur mused, as he leafed through the first pile Fister put before him. I'm going to make two piles, if you're agreeable… one of those I don't want to see again, the other for those I do."

They had moved to a back room, where file cabinets covered three walls, and another table took up the middle of the room.

They worked together easily, and without much conversation, Fister pulling and refiling as Trabur made his way through hundreds of pictures, holding one or two out of every fifty. As he'd boasted, the man did have a museum-sized library of material, having discarded nothing, it appeared, over decades of work in his field.

"Ah," murmured Trabur, one of his favorite expressions, "here's a classy lady."

"Who's that?" Fister wondered, moving behind the seated man to look over his shoulder. It was a portrait of Jessie Matthews in her prime, around 1935.

"I don't think many people in the states know who this British star was, but I do. I've seen all her movies. I've had a crush on Jessie Matthews ever since I first saw her on a 16 inch TV screen years ago. Even at that size, in fuzzy black and white, she was terrific."

"You're jesting!" Fisher exclaimed. "Not even many in this country remember her from those days!"

"She'll be in the American edition of your book, even if she doesn't appear in your British edition," Trabur asserted, "Have you got any more photos of her? Any of her dancing?"

"Why of course. Many. I handled all of her publicity for many years, you know. That was later, in the fifties."

Trabur went on in a relentless search for American stars or English stars well known to Americans, and found quite a few. By the end of this second day, he knew he'd already found enough to satisfy not only himself but his publisher at Galactic in New York. But he withheld that information from Fister. Let the man wait with a bit of suspense for now, Trabur decided, for no better reason than to keep him on his toes all the way through to the end.

So engrossed was he in his search that he hardly noticed when Fister excused himself to make a phone call in another room.

The fog persisted until early evening, so it was difficult to tell when the day was winding down, but this time Fister called a halt. "I won't accept any excuse tonight, Mr. Trabur. I want you to join me for dinner."

It was so commanding, so unlike most other pronouncements from the man that Trabur was taken aback and couldn't muster any excuse. The table was cleared, and within minutes they were motoring somewhere in Fister's modest automobile, a ten year old model of an English brand unknown to Trabur… but then, he didn't know one American car from another either.

It was a short trip, no more than twenty minutes from door to door, and they were still in the suburbs somewhere, though these outlying districts were not much like the single family homes common in the states. The streets of London seemed less crowded but the houses seemed moreso.

"There's someone I want you to meet," Fister said, and he seemed to chuckle as he stepped out of the car.

Trabur was ambivalent. Probably another wizened show biz crony from the old days, with more behind-the-scenes stories.

The door was opened by an attractive middle-aged woman, who smiled pleasantly as Fister made his introduction, "Mr. Trabur, this is Jessie Matthews."

Chapter 9

Cecil and Goyings can't get along

"It's a little late to be messing about in the kitchen, Mr. Goyings," Cecil had a look of disdain on his face, and a pistol in his hand.

"So what. I missed dinner, on a last minute trip for the old man, so I fixed a sandwich with leftovers. Is that a crime?" He yawned widely, chair tipped back on its two back legs, with his feet on the table.

"It's after midnight!" Cecil spit out the words as if an unforgivable rule had been violated. He was in his robe and slippers, having already retired to his bedroom for the night.

"Yes, it's after midnight. I thought vampires like you were most active at this hour." Goying's comment was uttered in a quiet, controlled tone, which he knew annoyed Cecil even more than when he displayed his own temper.

"If I find any sign of this… rummaging… in the morning, you'll be dismissed!"

"Stuff it, Cecil. You don't scare me."

"Humpft!" was Cecil's response, as he retreated to his room.

Goyings finished his meal, and tidied up, but not very fastidiously. That's what the maids were paid to do.

'I'm going to kill that man someday' he vowed to himself, and it wasn't an idle bluff. The two men, forced to live under the same roof, absolutely detested one another, and the situation had reached a tense standoff.

Chapter 10

A genuine star, still in earthly form

FISTER HELD COURT OVER DINNER, and Trabur was happy about that. He was feeling less nervous as the evening wore on, but still in awe of their companion, who, though surely over 60, still carried herself, if not regally, at least with a dignified posture and grace. Jessie Matthews in the flesh, a vital woman with the same engaging smile that had won him over through grainy black and white film on an old TV set many years before. Her starring days were long past, which seemed not to bother her overmuch. She made no fuss about it, joking and laughing at her own expense, urged on by the prodding of the ever jovial Fister, who remembered everything about everybody, it seemed. The years had treated the woman as indifferently as everyone else, with a few highs and more lows that lasted longer, but all that was only superficially explored at this first meeting. It was a time for modest merrymaking, for Trabur the happy occasion of meeting someone he admired greatly, for her the pleasant realization that a professional man from the United States not only knew who she was, but was an unabashed fan. But most of all it was a coup for Lywellen Fister, a reminder to himself that he was still in the celecbrity game.

By the time dessert arrived, Trabur had recovered his confidence, thanks in great part to the friendly attitude of Miss Matthews. She was as charming in real life as he'd imagined she would be, not at all impressed with herself, but then she didn't have to be because he so obviously was. The years receded in his eyes until she took on the image of the grand movie star she once was.

Drinks had accompanied the meal, and all three were gaily tipsy by now. The name of Noel Coward was brought into the conversation.

"Noel Coward wrote one of the most beautiful songs I ever heard." Trabur found himself saying.

"Which song was that." Jessie inquired. They were on a first name basis by this time, except for Fister. To them both he remained Mr. Fister.

"I've forgotten the title, but I used to be able to whistle it, for some reason," Trabur babbled, "I don't know why. I never tried to whistle any other song."

"Go ahead," she prodded, "Maybe I can guess the title."

"Oh, I haven't done it for years," he protested, suddenly embarrassed.

But she insisted. He looked around at the surrounding tables. There were few other patrons in the place, and none very close. He thought about it for a minute, wondering if a single sound would come out of his mouth, but the liquor had loosened his inhibitions, and suddenly he was whistling softly, slowly, the melody coming back to him somehow, magically it seemed to him in retrospect later, when he thought about it.

Jessie Matthews listened raptly, with a look of surprise on her face, and nodded, encouraging him to stay with it. Just as he recalled, each passage led to the next, straight through to the end. When he finished, she clapped gleefully, which did finally gain the attention of the others in the restaurant. The waiter hustled to their table, anxious about any possible problem with his service, but she shooed him away with a dismissive wave of her hand.

"You're spot on, old chap, every note, even the verse! Are you a musician, Robert?" She was definitely impressed.

"Oh no. I had to play in my school band as a kid, but it was the French horn, and I hated it. I don't know anything about music."

"Well, you're right. That was a Noel Coward song. 'Someday I'll Find You'. It was a big hit here in England during the war years. World War Two," she clarified, realizing it was just one historical war now, not the Big War of her generation. "But I didn't know it was known at all in the states. After all, you had Cole Porter, Irving Berlin and the Gershwins…"

"I heard it often on the radio, but I can't recall now who sang it. I don't think it was Coward himself."

Fister sat complacently, listening to their exchange. It was the first time all evening either of them had gotten in more than a few words between his stories, jokes and general spieling. The night was a success, and he felt amply satisfied, even more satisfied when Trabur picked up the check.

The ride back to Miss Matthews home was capped off when she whistled a song herself, and they all laughed as Fister tried to produce one himself. Even his company was welcome, though Trabur tried to exclude him as he walked Miss Matthews to her door and bid her an effusive farewell, never expecting to see her again.

Chapter 11

A ditsy dame dines out

DEBRA WAS JUST ENTERING TONY'S Italian tavern, the Roman Restaurant, when she heard her name, and turned to see Chuck fast coming up behind her.

"You're just in time," he enthused cheerfully.

"Just in time for what?" she went along with his line, pretty sure she knew what he had in mind.

"Just in time to join me for dinner, of course."

She'd guessed right, but couldn't think of any excuse she could make to get out of it.

'Well, I guess I am,' she responded with a smile, as she proceeded through the front entrance, followed one step behind by the amorous salesman from her apartment building.

'Well, what the hell', she thought to herself. It wouldn't inconvenience her to share a meal with the fellow. At least his company would keep Tony, the owner of the place, from bothering her.

She went directly to a booth toward the back, where the traffic wasn't too heavy, and took a seat. Chuck slid in across from her, acting as though it had been a pre-arranged date.

"Where have you been all day?" he asked, as if he had a right to know. "I didn't see you at the pool."

"I was working in the city."

"Working? Did you get a job?"

She wondered just how much she wanted to tell this character about her life, and took a couple of minutes to decide as the waitress appeared with menus and a short recitation of the specials available.

"I'll have the ham steak and mixed vegetables. Skip the potato. And coffee." Debra didn't need to look at the menu.

"No cream, right?" The waitress had a good memory, even for semi-regulars.

"That sounds good," Chuck piped up, "but I'll have a baked potato with it."

The girl got the rest of Chuck's order, and skipped away.

Debra spotted Tony, who was looking her way, but trying not to. Good. She'd act friendly with Chuck and be able to tell Tony at a later occasion that he's her steady guy. She gave the lug a big smile.

"So tell me about your job," he prodded.

She told him all about it, and he appeared to find it fascinating. He threw in a few salacious jokes, but she just ignored that, and they both enjoyed their meals.

Debra made a half-hearted attempt to pay for her own dinner, but as she knew he would, Chuck insisted it was his treat.

"If it weren't so late, I'd suggest we go dancing," he said, as they made their way to the street.

"It is late, but you can walk me home if that's where you're going." She might as well be pleasant, realizing there wasn't any way she could prevent that either. But she did cut the evening short when they reached the lobby of their apartment building. Offering a hand to shake, she was polite without offering any encouragement at all.

"Goodnight, Chuck."

"Goodnight, Debra. How about—"

"I'll be seeing you," she didn't let him finish, just hit the stairs at a trot, throwing a waffling wave of her hand.

Chapter 12

Over and done and gone

THE WORK WENT SMOOTHLY, AND only two days later Trabur had selected almost 200 photos, posters, assorted playbills and esoterica for use in the US edition of Fister's book. He made copies of the fellow's rough layouts and edited his copy, allowing for the proper English phrasing when necessary. The actual preparation of the two editions would be done simultaneously in the New York offices, but his work here was finished. He'd still have four or five days to explore London and whatever other English locales he wished to see before the long flight back home to New York. He thanked Fister for his hospitality, but gave the impression he'd be leaving the city the next day.

All of his plans evaporated after a brief telephone call to his hotel room that evening. He was plotting a course on a map of the British Isles, startled by the unexpected ring.

"Mr. Trabur," a familiar voice purred, "This is Jessie Matthews."

"Well, hello," was all he could say.

"How's the job going?"

"All finished."

"I was wondering if you'd like to pop in again?"

Talk about an explosion of ideas racing along the neurons of Robert Trabur's mind! What could this woman have in mind? Was it romance? Sex? Business? Yes, of course... some kind of business. All this and more was considered, but only a fraction of a second passed before he drawled amiably "I'd love to."

Arrangements were made. Directions by car were carefully written down, and a time and date were set. Though she hadn't said anything one way or another, he'd gotten the impression she was between engagements. She'd been busy on a daily TV soap opera for years, he'd learned, but that had ended some months before, and she was currently in negotiations about appearing in a play of some sort. She was still active in show business, though at a more modest level than in her starring movie years three decades before. Like most actors, she accepted character roles as she matured, relinquishing the spotlight to the fresh young faces that turned up regularly to thrill the public.

That was it, of course. She'd written an autobiography, a book like all others of that type, in which she was the center of the universe, and everyone she'd met from birth to the present revolved around her. A Mae West story.

Well, not to dismiss it without reading it, he decided. She hadn't seemed overly egocentric upon their first meeting. Perhaps she had a realistic view of the world, and her place in it.

Or maybe it was something entirely different. Something exotic...

Their date was for Sunday morning. Late morning.

There was a whole Saturday in between. He'd already inquired about renting a car, and took it out the next morning for a day trip around the city and well beyond. He enjoyed the sights, though he had to concentrate on driving the wrong side of the road. It wasn't too difficult except when turning, and there were a few close calls, but he arrived safely back at his hotel before dark. Now there was nothing to do except wonder what was in store for him the next day.

He looked at his watch. Seven PM. He'd had enough of British TV over the previous two evenings. A lot of it was much like the standard fare in the USA including reruns of already discontinued American dramas. There must be something else for an upstanding young buck to do on a Saturday night. Robert Trabur was certainly a socially conservative fellow, but he wasn't backward.

His first stop was the hotel bar, next to the lobby.

Chapter 13

Cecil and Goyings go at it

Goyings was drenched, washing the truck, when he heard the intercom phone ring in the garage. He decided to ignore it and finish the job. Then he'd change into a dry shirt and trousers, and go see what it was about.

But Cecil swooped through the door into the garage, and out to the courtyard, within a couple of minutes. "Did you hear your phone, Goyings?" He'd stopped addressing him as Mister Goyings, no longer attempting to maintain a polite relationship.

"Yes, I heard the phone. I thought I'd dry off before entering your sacred domain to find out what I've done wrong now."

"You're a sluggard. When the phone rings, you're to answer immediately, no matter what you're doing. It might be an emergency!"

"An emergency..." he mumbled, "Everything seems to be an emergency for you lately."

"There's a job for you!"

"What's on the agenda?" He ignored the insult, though it registered.

"I want you in proper uniform and the Rolls full of petrol by seven PM."

"You want? You don't want anything. You're delivering a message." Goyings could feel the blood rushing to his head, "You're just a trained puppy, Cecil, that's all you are. You don't outrank me around here, so sod off and go back to your feather dusting."

But Cecil couldn't let it go at that. He despised this rude scoundrel who stomped around in his leather boots as though he was entitled to every luxury and comfort of the house... the house he, Cecil, tried so hard to maintain in pristine condition at all times.

"I'm preparing a detailed record of your infractions, you scurvy tramp. Your days here are num-"

The water in the hose, at a low pressure, could still reach Cecil when Goyings pinched the nozzle with his thumb, which is what he did. The stream hit the officious prig in the face and chest, a perfect bull's-eye!

"You stupid git!" he howled, backing away as fast as he could.

Goyings just laughed. Now he wouldn't have to let a headache ruin the rest of his day.

Chapter 14

The whole mob goes to the movies

ROBERT DROVE CAREFULLY, FOLLOWING THE directions his new friend Jessie Matthews had provided, and pulled into an open parking space near her townhouse, suspicious but still eager to know why she wished to see him again, trying to convince himself it would be a letdown, whatever it was.

She opened the door dressed modestly but a bit more carefully put together than he'd last seen her, with hair neatly coiffed, earrings, a bracelet, rings and make-up including extra eyelashes and a lovely orange lipstick, all of which subtracted another decade from her true age. If this was all for him, Robert wasn't sure he was prepared. He was relieved to find a few other people present, most of them not dressed as fashionably as she was, few of them very forbidding at first sight. She introduced them each by name and their association with her. Most seemed to be contemporaries from her starring movie days, like her hairdresser (well, that explained her appearance this morning), her stand-in, who did resemble her, her current agent, with a funny name she wouldn't forget, Gordon Feastwell, son of the agent she had back in the good old days, and a tall middle-aged man who did seem a little more rough and weathered than the others.

"This is Sonnie Hale," she said cheerily, "Among other distinctions, he was my second husband." They shook hands, and Robert winced at the tight grip the man exerted. He didn't give even the hint of a smile.

Although Robert couldn't know anything about it, Feastwell had alerted Jessie that Hale had turned up after many years, and mentioned he'd like to see her. She didn't want to meet him alone, which was a second reason for the assemblage today. She figured she could talk with Sonnie without getting into anything too personal surrounded by so many others in a group.

The only other man in the crowd who looked a bit out of place was a Mr. Poundstack, dressed fashionably in an expensive suit, well fitted to his stout middle-aged figure, topped with a Homburg hat worn like a crown. As it turned out, the man did have pretensions to a royal place in British society, but Robert wouldn't know about that until later.

While the introductions were being made, the doorbell rang again, and in slithered a voluptuous younger woman with a silly name, something like Natasha Bugner. She was a more recently acquainted fellow actress from the daily TV series.

"We're going to the movies, my dears," Jessie declared, without further explanation, as they all started making their way out the door. A caravan of three cars were needed to transport the crowd, which got a little more crowded as two other revelers were picked up along the way.

Robert was directed to Poundstack's grand black limousine. The well-padded proprietor took up most of the back seat, with Robert and Jessie on either side. The only person occupying the front seat was Poundstack's chauffer, a sober character he called Max, crisply uniformed in shades of gray, with a matching gray hat.

The now more impressed American took a good look at the large man beside him. He seemed poised enough, even a bit arrogant, but there were beads of sweat on his forehead and droopy jowls. He didn't appear dissipated in any obvious way, but well beyond his prime.

"Are you in show business too, Mr. Poundstack?" Robert inquired, as they made their way leisurely along the busy London boulevards.

"No," he replied, without offering any alternative, "I'm just Miss Matthews' greatest fan. That's what I considered myself until you appeared, Mr. Trabur."

"I'm sure there are thousands of us," Robert was quick enough to say, "She's a great star all over the world."

"You're both liars," Jessie blurted, with a laugh that proved she didn't mind their bombast at all.

When they reached their destination, an antiquated movie theater with for rent signs prominently displayed around the front of the building, another dozen people were waiting expectantly on the sidewalk. It was all a bit perplexing to Robert, even moreso when one of the others remarked to him as they filed into the dim theater, "This is all for you, Mr. Trabur. A rare viewing of a classic movie. It's been donkey's years since it was last shown."

It all seemed clear to this stranger, and since all of them were in such a jovial mood, he allowed himself to share in it, without feeling as stressful as he usually did when he wasn't sure what was going to happen next.

Jessie Matthews was clearly the center of attention, and enjoying herself. She went directly to the seat she wanted to occupy and motioned Robert to take the one beside her. The others settled nearby in little clusters, and within a few minutes the lights dimmed even more than when they'd entered. There weren't any more clues to what was about to be shown, but when the old black and white print, fluttered and frail, began to throw its stuttering images on the screen, Robert realized everybody was looking at him with big grins on their faces.

For good reason. The look of surprise on his face must have been very entertaining. The title 'Dancing Partners' was followed by 'starring Fred Astaire and Jessie Matthews'. He read the remaining credits without any of them registering except for 'music and lyrics by Noel Coward'. And then the film broke and the screen went black.

"I was afraid of this," Jessie muttered softly, "This old print is about to fall apart completely."

"What IS this?" was all Robert could say.

Everybody was jabbering in the background, but he paid close attention to Jessie as she explained "Remember when you said I should have made a movie with Fred Astaire? I almost blurted it out right then, but then I thought no, I'd get the old gang together for a screening. It's been years since we've run it, just for giggles."

"But I never heard of this movie," Robert interrupted.

"I haven't either." It was Poundstack, on Jessie's other side, and he looked as stunned as anyone present. A quick survey by Robert indicated he wasn't the only one there who knew nothing about Jessie's big revelation.

"Oh, it was never released. Not even here in England. It was just a lark, really, but it got out of hand. Everybody wanted to be a part of it, and it ended up a full length movie, with comedy acts and bits of business just like in the real Astaire movies."

"That's incredible!" Robert blurted, a true expression of his amazement.

"Jessie, how could you have kept this from me?" Poundstack betrayed his genuine jealousy with that remark, it seemed to Jessie's new Yankee admirer. The old rogue really did think he rated the number one place in her list of champions.

A voice called out from the projection booth, "I think I've got it ready to roll, Jessie." The lights dimmed again, and the movie started, jittery at first but proceeding smoother as it went along. Robert was all at attention, catching every scene in his memory, believing this was probably a once only chance to see this rare footage. The sound was really tinny, and the thick English dialects were so alien to American pronunciations that he could scarcely make any sense of the dialogue, but the story wasn't at all hard to follow. It was a typical light-hearted 1930's musical, right down to the graceful costumes and lush settings that showed a world that never existed in reality anywhere on earth.

At one point, someone yelled out, "There you are, Sonnie!", there was a spattering of applause, and Robert tried to discern which of the thin young men on the screen was the same hulking brute he'd met earlier.

The rest of the audience were thoroughly enjoying the movie, with frequent outbursts of laughter, and Robert joined them, all the while marveling at the lilting music and tricky choreography as Fred and Jessie gracefully danced... he in top hat and tails, of course, and she in a diaphanous backless silk gown that displayed her curvy figure to full advantage.

When they turned to check each other's reaction, Robert whispered excitedly, "This is wonderful!", and she smiled broadly.

The film broke again, several times, but after a few brief interruptions, finally made it all the way to the end. Wild applause followed the conclusion, and Robert joined in that too.

He was speechless, glad the others surrounded the glowing star as she accepted their praise. The merry mood of the crowd was subdued when the projectionist joined them and announced solemnly, "I'm afraid that's the last time we'll be able to run it, Jessie. It's falling to pieces."

"We're all going back to my place for a drink." Jessie announced after they'd all filed out to the street, "and that includes you, Mr. Trabur."

He followed along, included now as a member in good standing of Jessie's loyal fan club, and a good time was had by all.

Chapter 15

Goyings suffers

DINNER FOR THE STAFF WAS normally late, around eight PM, but it wasn't unusual for exceptions. Goyings, the chauffer, showed up after ten one evening, just in from bringing the master back home after a day in the city.

"Any chance of anything hot at this hour, Murphy? He asked the Irish cook, who was still on duty, already preparing something for the next day.

"There's some beef stew. I can warm it up in ten minutes."

"That sounds fine. I'm knackered, but I need a bit of something. I'll change out of my uniform and be right back."

He saw Cecil, down the main hall, on the way to his room, but neither of them acknowledged the presence of the other. They rarely spoke unless it was absolutely necessary.

The stew was not very good, and he threw half of it in the garbage, careful not to let Murphy see him do it. Normally he was a fairly good cook, and a buddy. The doughnut for dessert was enough to satisfy his appetite.

Almost as soon as he got to his room, his stomach started sending distress signals. Had Murphy served him rancid meat? He took a couple of acid reducing pills, and got into bed, figuring to watch TV for awhile. Oh, the BBC had already signed off for the night.

The pills weren't helping yet, so he decided a beer might set things right. There were a couple of cold bottles in his mini-fridge. The malt seemed to settle his innards, so he downed the second bottle too, and went back to bed.

As soon as he was prone, the pain shot from his stomach to his chest, and got worse. Much worse. Moments after the flash fear of a heart attack, he realized he was about to heave. He staggered to the bathroom where all the beer, all the stew, and whatever he'd had for lunch as well, came out in several convulsive eruptions.

After it was over, he cleaned his face, took a few sips of water, and crawled back to his bed. The pain persisted. He lay there, moaning, unable to do anything but grit his teeth and wait for the throbbing to subside. After a long hour, it finally did.

'Where the hell did that come from?' he finally regained enough lucidity to wonder. Food poisoning, what else could it be?

Wait a minute. Food poisoning from Murphy's home-cooked stew? If there'd been a problem with it, surely the rest of the staff who'd eaten it hours earlier would have had the same symptoms.

And then it hit him. He sat upright in his bed! Cecil! Cecil had put real poison in the stew he knew was being prepared just for him!

The villain had made his strike! Goyings didn't feel up to confronting the scoundrel then, in the wee hours of the morning, when any disturbance would awaken his employer as well as the rest of the household. Yet without doubt, the daft old plonker had gone too far now!

Goyings finally got to sleep, but not before he'd imagined several unpleasant fates for the malevolent butler.

Chapter 16

A marvelous plan

THE MORE HE THOUGHT ABOUT it, the more convinced Robert was that destiny had placed himself in this city for a far more important reason than the one his employer had sent him to do. 'Dancing Partners' had been such a revelation for him that he realized it could be for millions of others. He knew he had to persuade Jessie Matthews to share it with the world. Apparently it had been such a trivial aside to her own career at its height that she still kept it in that private place in her memory, but Fred Astaire, now that was an altogether different matter. Fred Astaire really was a living icon. Composers still slipped his name into modern lyrics, and his fame endured worldwide despite the years that had passed since he put away his dancing shoes. The news that a never-before-seen Fred Astaire musical movie from the 1930's existed would be a sensation!

His business with Fister had been completed, and he still had a few days grace before the flight back to the states. All thoughts of seeing the London sights and engaging in the usual tourist activities vanished from his mind as he fixated on his new mission.

Jessie Matthews seemed pleased to hear from her American fan again, when he called the next day. It had to be an evening appointment because she'd spent the day auditioning for a play, the name of which she hadn't bothered to memorize since it was still an amorphous project, one of many she'd considered over the years, many more in fact than those that were actually produced for a paying public. She didn't resent having to prove her ability to play the character as written, aware enough in her maturity to understand some characters are simply beyond one's talents no matter how many credits filled a resume. But she was stressed after a long day in make-up, the object of several poker-faced producers' close scrutiny, and had already finished a stiff drink by the time Robert knocked on her door.

The idea of releasing the film had occurred to her years before, when she read in the trade papers that Astaire's exclusive contract with RKO had expired, but that was during World War Two and musicals were as obsolete in England as silent films during the 40's. None of the executives she approached with the project even wanted to see it, much less release it. The years passed until eventually she considered it so dated, and so clumsily made, that it was silly to pursue the idea.

But Robert went into salesman mode, a skill he'd acquired selling encyclopedias for a couple of years before landing his job at the esteemed Galactic Publishing Company. He pressed a couple of positive outcomes, then relapsed into totally unrelated subjects over a leisurely dinner until she brought back the topic of Dancing Partners herself over dessert. Another positive outcome was provided, something about the money such a film might generate, and Robert followed that up with "You don't have to do a thing. I'll handle it for you, free of charge except expenses, and those to be paid only after it's in the hands of a legitimate distributor. I'll get signed permission from Astaire and all the others involved."

Jessie Matthews was all smiles for the rest of the evening, which consisted of her driving Robert back to his hotel.

"I'll leave it all to you, Robert," she said softly, close to his ear as he prepared to exit the car. He felt a shiver, standing there on the street as she went on her way. It wasn't the first time she'd used his first name, but the emphasis on the way she whispered it had the impact of a kiss. The lady's charms, just below the surface, were still potent when she chose to release them. There would have to be a contract between them, of course, but he'd made the sale. Now all he had to do was figure out how to make it all come true.

Chapter 17

A would-be Royal lives grandly

Mortimer Poundstack was beside himself and that was too much of him to fit in any room, so the two of them went outside and walked the grounds of his estate without a destination, ignoring the sights and sounds of his surroundings. Voices were pestering him, and they were all his. Seeing that old movie with Jessie at her loveliest and most enchanting had revived in him an adoration of intensity he'd not really had since first discovering her as a callow youth a generation, or was it two, so much earlier in his life.

She didn't seem to understand the implications of this old relic, but he realized it could be major. It was like discovering the tomb of Tutankhamun. Treasures the world never knew existed were there in the decaying frames of the fragile old motion picture she possessed.

By nature a selfish, cold and calculating man, Poundstack held a pure and unwavering admiration of Jessie Matthews. The half-brother of a genuine duke, he'd inherited the duke's land and palatial home early in life, everything except the title, an insult that still festered. His revenge had been to use his power and position to acquire even more power and a grander position, one that placed him in his own estimation higher on the social scale than most of the certified dukes of the kingdom. He had farms and orchards, a collection of art and antiques to rival most museums, and, his most prized possessions, a stable of fine racehorses.

At the sturdy age of 62, Morris Poundstack had everything he wanted except one, the hand of Jessie Matthews in marriage. She was a genuine friend, but had said no several times, more times than he cared to remember, and it gave him ulcers to deal with that stalemate. He truly was the woman's greatest fan, and it was the old reprobate's almost but not quite one hundred percent unselfish regard for her that he wondered now how he could help her capitalize on this unexpected turn of events.

There wasn't any opportunity to talk to her after the movie was shown, which was probably just as well because he didn't know how to react or what to say. He'd tried to telephone the day after, but was unable to reach her by ten PM and knew better than to call after that. Early in their relationship she'd made it clear he wasn't to call before noon either, and he followed her rules without argument. She was a moodier-than-most moody woman, but her life had been filled with drama and desperation between her triumphs, so her stalwart protector was understanding and patient. He knew a history like hers would have made anybody at least a little bit edgy. Poundstack made himself busy with various chores to pass the time, but the wait seemed interminable. When he finally reached her, he was too late to take the initiative. The American had already made his move, and Jessie appeared more than satisfied.

"Mr. Trabur will take what remains of the print to the states and have it repaired, restored somehow, before he takes it to Fred Astaire personally to get his authorization to have it released. Can you imagine? After more than 30 years!" Jessie seemed thrilled with the idea now, totally convinced it was a great idea.

Poundstack listened, sensed her enthusiasm and realized it would be difficult to steer her on a different course, but tried anyway. "Jessie, you don't know this man! You just met him! He could be a confidence man!" Poundstack knew how a cultured man could present himself as morally sound, all the while scheming shamelessly. He was a master himself at that game.

"Oh, Mortimer! He's harmless, very gentle and sincere." Jessie had been married to three manipulative men, and involved one way or another with dozens more. She thought she now had a pretty savvy appreciation of any man's character within a short span of time. That's why she'd said no all those times to Poundstack. He was a dependable, generous attendant but she suspected he would be a louse as a husband.

"Jessie, you can't let that film out of your hands unless you're positive it will get back to you safe and sound", he declared emphatically.

She paused long enough that he followed that up with an improvised, impetuous "You must assign someone you know and can trust to accompany Mr. Trabur every step of the way, to have possession and guard that film!"

She paused again, while Poundstack took a minute to wonder what he was proposing.

"Well, who would that be?" Jessie asked.

"Don't make another move until you hear from me, Jessie. He hasn't got the print yet, has he?" He was stalling for time, unable to come up with anything else on the spur of the moment.

"No. I've still got it."

"I'll call back in an hour. Will you be home?"

"Yes, I'll be here. But I think you're overreacting, Mort."

"I'll call you in exactly an hour," he said forcefully, and hung up the phone, uttering a loud "Blast!" that brought the butler into the room.

"Are you alright, sir?" he inquired solicitously.

"I'm not, but there's nothing you can do about it, Cummings." He was the most efficient butler Poundstock ever had, so he was careful not to alienate the man needlessly.

Chapter 18

A junior miss Jockey is drafted

CASSANDRA THIMBLE BROUGHT HER FAVORITE mare, the petite Amanda, into the yard at a trot, and jumped off, pleased as usual, after her regular morning ride. Shlug Mugger was there to take the reins and walk the horse around slowly until she was breathing normally and ready to enter her stall in the stable.

"Cummings called a few minutes ago, Casey. Your uncle wants to see you." He delivered the message casually, but knew she'd be annoyed. She had dinner almost every evening with her uncle, and they didn't have any problem conversing then about any subject. It meant something serious whenever he summoned her during the day, and whatever he had to say on those occasions was inevitably bad news for her.

So she stomped off toward the main house. She knew exactly where she'd find her uncle, and there he was, standing by the fireplace in his study, making a production of cleaning out his pipe and dumping a few ashes into the growing pile of them behind the screen.

"How would you like to have a holiday... take a trip?" he inquired in a tone that was more of a declaration than a question.

It was just his manner, but it irritated her anyway. Why couldn't he ask her something like that as if he cared if she said yes or no? So her defenses were up from the start.

"What kind of a holiday?" she asked in a normal tone, not yet overly concerned.

"A trip to America. You've always been curious about the US, haven't you? What the Americans call a vacation." He repeated the suggestion to make sure she knew it was going to be fun, not work.

"What brought this on?" she asked, still prepared to believe it was something positive. Maybe there was a special horse in the states he wanted her to check out, perhaps purchase and ship back home.

"It's a long story. It will give you a laugh, I'm sure," he sat down heavily in his ornate chair beneath the gigantic framed portrait of Rosy Ribbon, the stallion that had been his champion of the year in 1963, the star attraction at the Newcastle racecourse in Gosford Park. Rosy Ribbon had been and still was the biggest moneymaker in his stable, even more valuable in stud than racing ever since his retirement. She decided to sit too, if this was to be a long story.

Chapter 19

Are these two really a couple?

AKBRAMIN MOISTING SAT AT HIS desk, munching still warm bits out of a basket of freshly delivered fish and chips. If the Americans could make money delivering pizza, why not try that gimmick in London. He had a 25% interest in the scheme, and all the chips he could eat. His girlfriend Sasha was supine on his couch across the room, in what appeared to be a natural position but which was actually a pose she often adopted for her still photos. She was dressed provocatively, but not too shocking for street wear in contemporary London, exactly the way Moisting wanted. He never got tired of looking at Sasha, and they both knew it was the bedrock reason they were together.

Moisting, twice her age, twice her weight, less than half as attractive and at least twenty times more wealthy, had no doubts at all about their relationship. He was the boss and she was his slave. She was free to leave anytime she pleased, and could probably even expect severance pay. He wasn't a total loser. But he did lack the capacity for genuine intimacy or commitment with another human being. There had been another slave before Sasha, and he was confident there would be another after she was gone, whenever that happened. Moisting read regional and international newspapers voraciously, sure the clue to his Big Score would turn up any day.

Meanwhile, he prospered as a producer who occasionally created legitimate films for various commercial accounts, but who was known primarily as an over-the-hill girlie film schlockmeister. Real pornography was burgeoning in the squalid low-life environs of England as well as every other democracy around the world, but Moisting wasn't up to that level of exploitation. Too much risk, both from the law and in other ways, for his lazy disposition. His sexiest entertainment consisted of busty girls stripping down to pasties and a G-string.

He'd always justified this product as the means to finance loftier ambitions, and did actually attempt to promote his most promising performers toward more prestigious careers. Sasha was one of those who had graduated from shaking her naked breasts on camera to actual speaking roles on radio and TV, Moisting's most accomplished client and grateful girlfriend. She wasn't illiterate, but didn't read or write, by choice, unless obligated to secure a role. She had no ambition at all, in fact, except to satisfy her aging impresario, who indulged all her whims and vices, the most expensive of which was shopping for clothes she rarely had occasion to wear. It never seemed to occur to her that her breasts would begin sagging as time passed, and the day would come when her body could no longer turn men to jelly. Live for today might be her motto, and she was lots of fun at a party.

Sasha and Ock, as she called him, what a pair and a pair. Meant for each other. This week.

"What were you doing yesterday? I didn't see you all day." He didn't really care, but she'd been sprawled there for twenty minutes waiting for him to acknowledge she'd entered his office.

"Went to a movie. A real rickety old movie. I went with my friend Jessie and a bunch of her friends."

"Jessie? Oh, that old gal. Was it one of her big pictures from the old days?"

"Before I was born, that's for certain. Everybody was talking about her costar... I think his name was 'Stair'."

"Stair?" Moisting's nose was back behind his paper, his beady eyes surveying the page three girl with knockers almost the size of Sasha's.

"Funny lookin' bloke. Big head, pointed chin, really skinny. But he was grand. He and Jessie were like a dream dancing together."

"Uh huh." Moisting muttered. Maybe he could match a page three girl with his Fish and Chips To Go somehow.

"Jessie told me she used to have a figure like mine, and I have to admit she was a knockout."

"Impossible, my luv. You've got the body of the century. I know. I've seen 'em all."

"Did you ever see any of her old movies?"

"Of course. Saw them when they were shown on TV in the '50's. She was a bit of alright. But I can't remember any of the dandies she danced with. I seem to remember most of the time she danced by herself." Moisting had tossed the paper and was putting on his shoes. He was on his way out but hadn't quite decided whether it was to be lunch with Sasha or a drink at the Royal Dungeon. He'd stuffed himself with chips all morning, so Sasha would have to find something else to do.

She was still running the movie in her short term memory, the only memory bank she could ever access halfway clearly, "Everybody was raving about Jessie and a stair. So I thought that must be his name."

Moisting almost dropped his shoe. "A stair? Astaire? Jessie Matthews never made a movie with Fred Aastaire."

"Maybe not. I wasn't paying much attention to it, except the dancing. I had more fun at the party later, at Jessie's place."

Chapter 20

Slinkring in the shadows

SOME PEOPLE THINK ABOUT THINGS other people never think about at all, things about how the universe evolved and how atoms arrange themselves into so many unique forms, from worms to elephants, sand to boulders, water to whiskey.

It's obvious, to those who choose to think about it, that dogs don't know how big they are in relation to other dogs. A little dog patrolling his own property can chase away a big dog loitering in the neighborhood because the big dog knows he's lost and doesn't belong there.

Human beings are a little more complicated. They know what they look like in relation to other people, and it has a lot to do with how they socialize or don't.

Asher Slinkring entered the lobby of his apartment building cautiously, his back against a wide wall while he scanned the general appearance and postures of the few others he saw there. Although not expecting trouble, he was always ready for it, alert to the threats and hazards of living in the big city. A large, ugly man, it was actually his own appearance that sent chills down the spines of most people he encountered.

Meeting Mr. Asher Slinkring face to face was a harrowing experience at best, a potentially traumatic experience if that meeting takes place in the dark, and there aren't any other people around. It had always been that way, since Asher's late adolescence, when that skull sculpted face on top of a six foot three inch, two hundred pound body entered a room without warning.

His frame had filled out considerably since then, of course, but it only heightened the total image of the man. Asher didn't find his face particularly frightening when he shaved, he'd grown accustomed to it, but the frightened expressions of those he met every day had made him paranoid and fearful of everyone and everything. The scared little boy inside the body of a monster had made him a paradox, a burly bartender and bouncer at the Royal Dungeon by night and a wretched solitary Quasimoto by day, writing poetry inspired by his romantic ideal, Miss Sasha Bugnum, who belonged to that miserable blowhard Moisting.

Moisting! Just the thought of the man enraged Slinkring! He hated everything about the gobby lard-arse, especially his arrogant personality and the disrespectful way he treated Sasha, treating her like a dog, even in public, with insults and threats of violence. If he ever struck Sasha in Asher's presence, he didn't know if he'd be able to control himself. Moisting didn't know how close he'd come to being seriously hurt by his callous manner with the woman secretly adored by the one everyone thought was a dead ringer for Doctor Frankenstein's spare parts creation.

He reached the safety of his humble apartment, and sat down to kick off his heavy shoes.

When the phone rang, Slinkring had to compose himself before answering. Recognizing his caller's voice immediately sent his blood pressure straight back up! "Slink, I've got a big job for you."

"I told you not to call me Slink, Mr. Moisting. I don't like it. I don't call you Achey or Mustard or Tingaling, but I will if you keep calling me Slink!" He was just worked up enough to pick a fight with the man.

"You're too sensitive. I wouldn't mind if you called me any of those things. Be creative. Call me Bastard Nuts if you want to."

"What kind of job? I won't beat anybody up, if that's the kind of job you're talking about."

"I never asked you to beat anybody up."

"No, but you wanted me to threaten somebody, and then he beat me up. I had to go to the doctor to have three stitches put in my nose. Do you remember that, Mr. Bastard Nuts?"

"I didn't know that chappy had been a professional boxer. I paid the doctor bill, didn't I."

"Every time I do something for you, I end up regretting it."

"Listen, Asher, this is a big job. I'm flying to America and I want you to go with me." He'd used Slinkring's first name, which he only did when he was pretending to be sincere.

"Not interested, whatever you have in mind."

"You're not interested in a free holiday to America?"

"It wouldn't be any fun. You'd have me doing some dirty job."

"Asher, I'll see you tonight and give you the belts and braces. Believe me, it will mostly be a pleasure trip. I'm taking Sasha too."

"... Sasha's going?"

"Of course. To America. You like Sasha, don't you? She's a lot of laughs."

"Well, I'll see you at the Royal Dungeon and listen, anyway."

Chapter 21

A Yank and a Brit, for better or worse

"You'll enjoy seeing Mr. Poundstack's palace, Robert," Jessie assured her companion, as they rode comfortably outside the city limits of London in the back seat of Poundstack's sleek black limousine. "The grounds are impeccably maintained, and his horses are simply majestic up close."

Robert tried to relax and take in the scenery but Poundstack's invitation seemed more like an order to appear, and that put a little suspicion into the journey. He'd made the trip to Jessie's place to take possession of 'Dancing Partners", but the imposing automobile was there waiting and Jessie hurried him into it as soon as he'd arrived. Had Poundstack somehow squelched the deal?

Max, the chauffer, was as professional and quiet as he was during Robert's previous trip in the car, but Robert knew he could hear their conversation, so he didn't ask any questions that might get back to the driver's employer. Homes and businesses grew more spare as they went along, and instead now there were open fields and orchards, most fenced in one way or another. Even twenty miles from the city limits, there appeared to be no large expanses of empty land, as there was surrounding most American cities. Robert assumed the country, smaller than the state of Texas, and centuries older, had subdivided every square inch by this time.

The grounds in front of Poundstack's property were every bit as grand as Jessie had described, and the palatial house was even more spectacular than he'd expected, almost a castle, probably at least a couple of hundred years old, more like a museum or a university building than a residence, it seemed to Robert.

The ornate door knocker brought a suitably sober butler to the door, and they were escorted along the main hall into Poundstack's library. The man himself was waiting for them there, and greeted his guests warmly. Greeting Jessie considerably more warmly than her escort, but that was certainly expected.

There was also a young woman in the room, one cheek of her buttocks perched on the edge of a large desk, one foot planted on the floor, obviously at home and at ease. She was chubby and plain, her hair a curly mess that looked like a buzzard's nest. She was wearing a torn sweater, baggy slacks, scuffed and battered boots. She couldn't have cared much about her appearance.

Poundstack introduced her as "Cassandra, my niece," without bothering to explain why she was in attendance. The girl nodded slightly but said nothing and faded into the background.

Cummings, the dignified butler, brought drinks on a tray as they were making small talk and Poundstack proudly showed off some of the more unique objects in his high-ceilinged, treasure-filled lair. Robert would have loved to spend a day or two going through the many shelves of books along the walls, but that wasn't the purpose of the meeting.

"We both have complete confidence in you, Mr. Trabur," Poundstack began, officiously, "but you'll be in possession of a very valuable one-of-a-kind artifact. I'm sure you realize that."

Well, of course he realized it. What did the man want, exactly? A cash deposit? His social security and bank account numbers?

"We feel," Poundstack continued, and again he was using that 'we' as if the film belonged to him as well as to Jessie, "that you should have a companion, Jessie's representative, to guard the film until it's returned to her."

"A guard?" Robert didn't like the sound of that.

"A traveling companion." Jessie interjected. She thought her input might be more reassuring, sensing Robert's hesitation.

"This is your idea, Jessie?" he asked her.

"I think it's a good idea. Just to be on the careful side. That way there won't be any accidents, losing the thing, or— "

Robert was wondering how he could afford to pay another round trip plane ticket, and meals, and...

"We'll take care of all the extra expenses, of course," Poundstack assured him, and in this case, Robert was sure he meant 'I'.

"Have you got somebody in mind?" he inquired, beginning to suspect they did. There was only one other person in the room, with no reason to be in on the conversation unless she was a part of the plan.

The portly man gestured at her as if calling attention to the latest model at a car show. "My ward, Cassandra. She's ready, willing and able, whenever you're ready to go."

Robert suddenly knew from personal experience what the word *speechless' meant.

"I've known Casey since she was a child, Robert." Jessie filled the void, "She's a very bright girl, and will be a big help to you in many ways, I'm sure."

Throughout the stilted conversation, Casey was making her own observations. This guy looked innocuous, even wimpy, she thought. Probably never rode a horse in his life. Or kissed a girl. Or worked up enough of a sweat doing anything to want to down a mug of beer in one long swallow afterward. She dreaded the trip even more now that she saw him than she had before her uncle laid down the law and told her she was going whether she liked it or not. She was sure it was going to be HELL from beginning to end.

Poundstack considered asking Casey to say a few words, but changed his mind when he saw her stoic expression, and sought affirmation from Robert instead.

"What do you say, Mr. Trabur?"

He tried to choose his words carefully. "If that's what you want, Jessie, it's okay with me. But I really don't think it's necessary. Nobody will know how valuable the package is, and I'll hold it on my lap or under my arm every step of the way until there are fresh new prints."

"Fine," Poundstack stood up and offered to shake hands, "let us know the day you want to leave, the departure time, and I'll make the reservations. Then I suggest we all meet at Jessie's place to transfer the reel of film, and my man will drive you both to the airport."

Chapter 22

Three in for dinner out

O N THE DRIVE BACK TO the city, Jessie suggested they go to one of her favorite restaurants for dinner, the Provence, in Chelsea, her treat. It turned out to be just the kind of place an old vaudeville trouper would like. She invited Max, the chauffer, to join them so he wouldn't have to wait in the car while they dined. The unspoken but still intact caste system of her country meant little to Jessie. She'd spent too many of her early years near the bottom so being at the top hadn't changed her appreciably. Rather than have Max take them back to her place, then switch to her car for the trip back to the restaurant, it seemed more logical to share their company with the usually chipper driver, who she knew well, having traveled hundreds of miles with, often the only passenger. She'd gleaned many insights into the character of her ardent suitor, Mortimer Poundstack, over the years, and they'd shared a good number of laughs together, but on this occasion he was out of character and turned out to be a bit glum and grumpy.

After ordering, the small talk didn't elicit any chuckles at all.

"You seem a bit down in the dumps, tonight, Max," she put a hand on his shoulder, her empathic nature coming to the fore, "Anything I can do?"

"It's a personal matter, Miss Matthews," he groused.

"Oh, well, if it's a personal matter, I won't—"

"It's that bastard, Cummings. He's set himself up in his mind three stations above mine, and I'm sick of it.

"Three stations...?" Robert was ignorant of the longstanding centuries old division of English society into levels of respect, from the King down to the lowly riffraff who populated the slums.

"Three stations, Max repeated, "He's been there far longer than I have, his wages are higher than mine, and he's in daily personal contact with our employer."

"You're alone with him a lot too, Max, aren't you?" Jessie was sympathetic, at least.

He thinks he's my superior, and does everything he can to bring me grief! I'm going to kill him if he doesn't lay off! I'll kill him!"

His outburst stunned them both.

"But... Cummings... he's such a docile fellow." Jessie couldn't imagine the reserved butler was anything like the bully Max was describing.

"He's two-faced, Ma'am, and extreme behind both of them." it appeared to be his last word on the subject, retreating into a stony silence as Robert and Jessie finished their meal.

It appeared Max needed one, but Jessie wouldn't let him have a drink because he was driving. Robert made up for it. He needed more than a couple to settle his own anxiety.

Chapter 23

Sasha and Asher get dressed

Sasha popped her head through the door of Ock Moisting's drab office with a puckish grin, and a melodic "Are you RED E?"

He didn't answer, but he did look up from his paperwork. Asher Slinkring. barely recognizable for a moment, stepped in, dressed as never before in a brand new dark gray suit, with a red vest, black shirt and white tie. Moisting took it all in, down to the shiny black shoes and back up to the pink rose in his lapel. "You're a vision, you are," he enthused, "You look like the chief pallbearer at the King's funeral."

Sasha followed him in, handing Asher the new bowler hat that made the costume complete.

"Better than I hoped," Moisting gushed, "Where's my change?"

"There isn't any change," Sasha plopped herself down on the couch, hardly bothering to arrange herself sensuously. "We couldn't even afford a cab back. Had to take a bus."

It had been Moisting's idea, so he couldn't complain. He knew Sasha, whatever her limits intellectually, would know better than he what a stylish uptown man should wear. Her taste in clothes was just right most of the time, well chosen for any particular occasion, but for everyday street wear, or in Moisting's company alone, she preferred short tight skirts and sweaters, the flashy togs of a tart.

"How do you feel?" he queried Slinkring, who looked so different, he must have some reaction.

"I feel pretty," said Slinkring, deadpan.

Sasha laughed at that. Moisting just shrugged. Everything was ready for the trip. They were to leave that night. She'd found out the departure time and airport in New York where Trabur and Casey Thimble would be arriving. Moisting, the day before, listening to Sasha's end of the conversation with Jessie, was sure no suspicions were aroused by her curious but subtle questions about Jessie's American admirer. Jessie, in fact, had told Sasha just about everything about Robert's expedition!

They would have to be there to meet the plane, identify Trabur, and follow him wherever he went. Sasha was the only one who knew what he looked like.

"You *will* be able to recognize him, won't you." demanded the overbearing Ock, her lumbering lover and psychological master.

"Yes, I *will* be able to recognize him," she imitated his emphasis-on-every-word delivery.

"We can't let him know he's being followed, whatever we do," he addressed Slinkring. "If they separate, we'll separate, but if we stay alert, an opportunity to grab that film will surely present itself."

Moisting had his own passport, and it wasn't difficult borrowing the others necessary from a couple of former employees, choosing them from his file of actors going back 20 years. The one for Sasha was easy, she looked like most of the other bimbos he'd used over the years, but Slinkring was definitely a unique character. He found a tall man, almost as repulsive, who at least looked enough like a brother, and hopefully nobody would be checking the photos too closely. All it took was a few pounds to get them in his hands. Sasha considered it a role, and memorized her character name. Slinkring, new to the acting profession, would take his cues from her.

Their bags were packed, last minute instructions were gone over once again, then Moisting called a cab, and they were on their way.

Chapter 24

Two bickering birds in flight

MISS THIMBLE AND MR. TRABUR sat starchly beside each other as their plane accelerated down the runway and soared into the sky above London, then quickly away over the ocean. It was the first time they'd been alone together, and neither had anything to say. They'd been paired in a complicated enterprise by others, and both were reluctant, to say the least. What had at first appeared to Robert as a potentially thrilling adventure had turned into the onset of a loathsome burden, and what had at first struck Casey as a loathsome burden seemed certain to go from bad to worse.

"Have you ever been to the United States?" he ventured limply, embarrassed by the silence between them.

"No," she replied, offering no help at all.

"I think you'll find it enjoyable... or at least interesting." he gave her a second chance.

"I know it wasn't your idea for me to tag along on this trip, so I'll try not to bother you," she finally said, in a flat monotone.

"Well, I hope so. It's up to you. You can pout all the way over and back, for all I care." Robert surprised himself by his abrupt comment, but he'd taken an affront by her taciturn attitude.

Pout? Was she pouting, she wondered.

It was a slow plod uphill from there. They understood each other's mutual disregard, so conversation was sparse and reserved for the rest of the flight. They took turns napping.

Chapter 25

Dingle Thimble at home

MEANWHILE, IN OTHER PLACES FAR and wide across the globe, plans and schemes were fomenting in the fevered imaginations of a varied ensemble of normally rational characters, including a hotheaded jockey named Shlug Mugger. Shlug, with his pockets full of coins, dialed a number he hadn't called for years from a public phone box a couple of miles from the Poundstack estate. He timed the call so that Dingle Thimble's phone would ring at 6:00 AM in Glendale California. It was the only time Shlug knew the old rascal would definitely be home in his bed, sober and alert enough to take a call.

"EH? What? Who is it?"

"It's Shlug, Dingle, calling from England."

"Shlug! How are ye, m'boy? What's wrong? Is Casey okay?"

"Casey's on a plane to America."

"A plane to America? It can't be true!"

"It's true, Dingle. I thought you'd like to know, and maybe you can get together."

"What's the story, Shlug?"

"I can't stay on the line long enough to give you the details, but sometime in the next week or so she'll be visiting the home of Fred Astaire."

"Fred Astaire? The dancer? I know who that is. I see him at the track sometimes. A fine gentleman, he is. But what would Casey be doin' with him?"

"She's got a special package for him. Some rare old film. I don't know much about it."

"Fancy that."

"How ya doin', Dingle?"

"I'm doin'."

"Me too. Look for Casey at Astaire's place."

"I'll do it."

"G'bye, Dingle."

"G'bye, Shlug."

They needn't linger on the phone. Dingle and his little protégé, Shlug, were regular penpals.

Chapter 26

Two of a kind, a kind too common

THERE WAS NOBODY IN AMERICA to welcome the arrival of Moisting, Bugnum and Slinkring. The well-tailored trio passed briskly through customs, delayed only slightly by Sasha's unusual variety of clothes and what turned out to be exotic perfume, then conferred over drinks in the airport lounge for a last review of their individual assignments.

Back in England, Gordon Feastwell was suffering from indigestion, constipation and hiccups. His misery had begun when his client, Jessie Matthews, revealed the long lost film she'd starred in with Fred Astaire. He'd done everything he could for a decade to keep that dizzy Matthews in show business, with limited success. How could she have kept this amazing secret from him, this secret worth who knows how much, in publicity alone! But Feastwell's greedy aspirations went well beyond that piddling pipe dream, all the way to the major prize, securing the exhibitor's license. So who was more worthy than he? Hadn't he protected her from that rusty rozzer Sonnie Hale? What he had to go through to keep them apart took diplomatic maneuvering beyond his pay scale, and he wasn't paid a shilling for it! Getting Jessie to put his name on a contract was one hurtle still to be accomplished when the time came, but for now there was only one simple scheme swamping his every thought. How could he get the film from that sappy American who'd strolled into Jessie's life like a bit player in a passing scene, and then taken over the lead without an ounce of effort or a hint of talent?

Ever eager, he'd already made two unsuccessful calls to Lew Murgin, his American associate, a relationship of very limited usefulness, but important occasionally, like now. Murgin apparently didn't even have a receptionist because the phone just kept ringing until he gave up and resolved to try again later. But Feastwell didn't have a receptionist either, so he could hardly feel superior by that measure. Twenty long minutes later, the persistent schemer dialed the number again, finally reached Murgin, and proceeded to fill him in on every detail of the perceived golden opportunity for both of them to hit the jackpot. They had nothing in hand, but quickly agreed it would be a straight 50/50 deal, after expenses. No paperwork between the two of them required. In the USA, London would be the official home office. In England and the continent, America would be calling the shots. At tax time, in previous ventures, the arrangement had been of great importance to both of them.

Murgin hung up the phone and sat staring into space for several minutes. A short man with a tall ego, his mind was racing. Feastwell's enthusiasm had carried all the way across the world to lodge just as fiercely in this mug's musings. For a guy who's whole life had been a slavering quest for the main chance, this looked like the real thing!

Who among his diverse list of talented performers could he possibly engage to be the point man in a possibly risky operation to secure that precious reel of film? Before long, the sinister features of his most cocky client came to the forefront of his consciousness.

He switched on his intercom. "Helen, get me Elisha Cook on the phone."

So, he did have a receptionist. But her voice was so rasping and unpleasant that he wouldn't allow her to answer the phone, no matter if he was in or out of the office. Many times, on the other hand, in his reception room, that same irritating voice was enough to send most unwanted visitors out before they got past her to annoy him.

Chapter 27

A wary couple triangu-
late in New York City

ROBERT AND CASEY HAD SETTLED into a cool truce. They didn't care for each other, but accepted their situation with professional cooperation. To Robert, Casey was a vulgar juvenile without any social graces, and in Casey's estimation, Trabur was a stuffed shirt with pudding in place of a brain, and no sense of humor at all. Each tried to maintain a reserved but respectful attitude toward the other.

Their relationship seemed a pleasant one to Robert's boss, Algin Fingerroth, the publisher and managing editor of Galactic Publishing Company, when they appeared in his office the next day after arriving back in New York. Robert had only given Fingerroth the merest hint of what he'd brought back, but since his superior was expecting nothing more than a report of his successful arrangement with Fister, the London based publicity agent, the distinguished executive was in a genial mood. He seemed quite taken by Casey, who, to her credit, was wearing a tastefully tailored blouse and slacks, sunglasses and a small bow in her closely cropped hair that seemed appropriate somehow. Her uncle Poundstack had made sure she had a first class wardrobe on this trip abroad. Even Robert had to acknowledge to himself that she presented herself well, which was an act of course, one she didn't bother to maintain with him alone. Since she always wore slacks, he figured she probably had hairy legs and was too lazy or indifferent to shave them. Or else she was bowlegged due to her years straddling broad-backed racehorses.

When Fingerroth's gracious welcome and Casey's demure charms had been established, Robert got straightaway to their important business of Jessie and Astaire's long lost film, and the potential for an important tie-in with Galactic Publishing.

The normally unflappable publisher, used to high-powered business discussions, listened, almost expressionless, but a few eyebrow arches and a slightly gaping mouth interspersed as the details were revealed betrayed his excitement. The Fister file, which Robert had brought along of course, was put aside for a later review, and a more expansive expense account was immediately arranged. No more serious confirmation was needed to place Robert and Casey on an open assignment for the company, to follow through on getting the fragile film transferred into a fresh print, and then to pursue its potential commercial value. Fingerroth himself would assist in every way he could, and Robert would write a firsthand account of the entire enterprise from beginning to end.

His own office was barely more than a cubicle, but there was room for Casey to sit near his desk as Robert made several calls. First he dialed Debra.

He had tried in vain to reach her the night before but she either wasn't home or wasn't answering the phone. Finally, she picked up. He couldn't tell her everything, but gave a glowing boastful account of his international business trip. Debra seemed indifferent to hear from him, scarcely aware he'd been out of the country, but that was her usual persona, so it didn't bother him.

Revealing few details but namedropping a few notables, Robert emphasized the news that he'd scored a coup for his company, and was well on the road to success.

Debra congratulated him.

He told her he wouldn't be able to see her for some time, perhaps for weeks.

She told him to keep in touch.

He hung up the phone with a broad smile, oblivious of Casey, who hadn't before seen that blissful expression on his face.

"She wants me to keep in touch," he mumbled, enjoying that thought for a few serene seconds before getting back to business.

The next call he wanted to make was to Fred Astaire's agent, in Hollywood, most likely, but it would probably take Fingerroth's secretary, Greta, who was also Robert's secretary when he needed one, some time to discover his name and a number where he could be reached. He put her on the trail, and told her he'd be back to the office later.

Casey had spent the night on his couch, but that was inconvenient, not to mention inappropriate for both of them, so the next thing to do was to find her a hotel room, somewhere close to the office or his apartment. Now that they had an expense account, that wouldn't be a problem at all. For the first time since they'd boarded the plane in London, they left the package containing Jessie's precious film in a closet in Robert's office and took to the streets with Robert carrying Casey's one small suitcase, she at last hands free.

Their mission was accomplished so quickly that they stopped for an early lunch in the hotel's restaurant, to give Greta enough time to accomplish hers. Neither of them ate very much because they'd had a full breakfast only a few hours before. At least Robert was acting a bit more spontaneous than he had before, Casey noticed, and seemed in a better mood.

When they got back to the office, Greta proudly turned over a name and phone number. He noted the name, then gave the number back to Greta. They agreed it would carry a lot more weight if a no-nonsense secretary introduced him to the man. He coached her quickly about exactly what to say.

After she got past the agent's secretary, he answered. "Hello, this is James Ames."

"Mr. Ames, Mr. Trabur of Galactic Publishing Company in New York is calling about a matter concerning your client, Fred Astaire."

"Yes, alright."

Robert took it from there. "Mr. Ames, I represent a lady named Jessie Matthews. Do you know who that is?"

"I don't believe so, no."

"Well, she was a major movie star in the 1930's, in England. Mr. Astaire knew her then."

"Yes... It's possible."

"I'd like to set up a meeting with you and Mr. Astaire as soon as possible."

"A meeting? No, I don't think so. What's this about?"

"It's about a movie called 'Dancing Partners'. That's all I can say just now. Mr. Astaire will remember that title, I'm sure. It's a matter that will involve a great deal of money..."

"A great deal of money... for your client, I presume?"

"Well, yes, and—"

"I'd prefer if you submit all the details in a letter. Do you have my address?"

"I have something to show Mr. Astaire. I assure you, he'll want to see it. A film with scenes of Mr. Astaire and my client, Miss Matthews. I'd like to have a meeting in person. I'm in New York but prepared to fly to California immediately."

There was a long pause, then "I'll relay your message to Mr. Astaire. Please give me your number and I'll get back to you very soon."

Robert gave the agent two numbers, the office and his own apartment number. Then, as an afterthought, he gave him Debra's number too.

Casey had followed Robert's part of the conversation closely, silently marveling at the difference between his professional business voice and the wavering, unsure stammering when he talked to his so-called girlfriend.

Chapter 28

Manhattan drama is laughable

ON THE STREET BELOW THE Galactic Publishing Company's offices, across from the front entrance, unobtrusively concealed from view were three suspicious characters named Moishing, Bugnum and Slinkring, waiting patiently for Robert and Casey to exit the building. They're on foot but their rented car is nearby, so they're prepared to separate if their two quarries do.

Gaining confidence by the hour, because there had been no problem at all, the unsuspecting pair were on to their next critical destination. The Facsimile Film Restoration Lab was located at a not very prestigious address, on lower Broadway, but it was a company recommended by a movie producer known to Algin Fingerroth, who had published the man's autobiography the year before. They were the best at their specialized trade, the producer assured Fingerroth.

Following the cab in their rented car, Moishing was sweating profusely and muttering cryptic Yiddish curses as he swerved back and forth in traffic, trying to remember which side he was supposed to be on, all the while keeping the other car in sight. At the very moment he realized he'd failed, Sasha, her nose almost attached to the windshield, yelled "They're getting out in the middle of the next block!"

They continued, as traffic made its herky jerky way along the busy boulevard, and saw Robert and Casey disappear into an entrance unknown, still far ahead. Sasha and Asher kept fixated on the spot, and exited the car, leaving Moishing to find a parking spot on the next side street.

The tall buildings along the street seemed all attached to each other by brick and mortar. Each entrance led to a small lobby with a board listing the businesses within. When Sasha spotted Facsimile Film, she was sure that was where Robert and Casey were headed. They checked the entrances on either side, but none appeared to have anything to do with movies. They quickly made their way to the nearest corner, and crossed to the other side of the streaming traffic along Broadway. Fortunately there was a large bookstore with tables of books bulging through the doors onto the sidewalk almost directly across from Facsimile Films, where they could mingle idly without any danger of being spotted.

Moishing joined them shortly before Robert reappeared, without Casey, and hailed another cab.

"She's remaining with the film while they work on it," Moishing groaned, "I was hoping they'd leave it. It would have been a snap to—"

"It would have," grumbled Asher, "But it isn't. They haven't left that bloody film out of their hands since they boarded the plane at Heathrow!"

"You two stay here," Moishing ignored Asher's outburst, and noted the name of the bookstore. "I'll pick you up at midnight if she doesn't come out before then."

"Midnight?" It was Sasha's turn to explode. "You expect me to stand around here until midnight?!"

"Think about all those days and nights lounging at the world's finest resorts when we've made this score!" He turned and left, trotting along pretty fast for a fat man, before they could come up with any more complaints.

Moisting's intuition was exactly correct. Casey alternated between sitting primly in Tucker Goodman's outer office, then strolling back occasionally to his cluttered workroom to watch him go through the procedures to transfer the old film into a fresh print that wouldn't fall into pieces as it clattered through a projector. It seemed to be a complicated job, so she didn't resent the hours passing with little for her to do except to close her eyes and let her mind imagine more satisfying pursuits. She was young, the future offered myriad opportunities, so even staying within the possible, it wasn't difficult to fantasize. She'd just settled into a tasty romance with a dashing American cowboy backstage at the rodeo when she was interrupted by Tucker Goodman's sudden arrival at her side, with a casual proposal.

"How about going out for a bite?"

"A bite?" She left the rodeo abruptly, her cowboy vanished, and she wondered what Goodman had in mind...

"I can't finish this today," he explained, "There are just too many patches and breaks. We could get something to eat, then I'll put in a couple more hours tonight."

"You can't work straight through?" Casey wondered.

"No way. You'll have to come back for it tomorrow."

"Can I take the film with me?"

"The original film is in pieces. It will be safe here tonight."

Casey sighed. She'd promised her uncle not to let the film out of her sight.

"I'll stay right here tonight," she asserted, without equivocation, "Maybe there's a pizza place that could deliver?" She had a random memory of someone telling her such businesses had been invented in the United States.

"You're sure one stubborn young lady, but if that's the way you want it, so be it," Goodman relented, letting his own little fantasy evaporate.

Chapter 29

An anti-climactic Manhattan climax

Dusk had turned Manhattan's streets into a stark pattern of dark shadows below the lingering sun dappled upper stories of the tall buildings in every direction as Sasha and Asher paced and dawdled along Broadway, glumly carrying out their surveillance mission, trying to escape the notice of anyone, like the lone policeman they saw patrolling by foot and anyone else who stared at them for any length of time. They'd seen the Party Pizza man make a delivery into the building they were watching, and grabbed him on his way out to put in an order for themselves. It was obviously going to be a long night.

When Robert showed up mid-morning the following day, in response to Goodman's phone call, Casey was too fatigued even to complain. Robert admired her dedication to the job, though he considered it a bit extreme. He would have left with Goodman when he locked up for the night, but she'd spent the night on a couple of hard chairs in his waiting room. Now the job was through, and Robert was determined to make this day more pleasant for his loyal partner.

Goodman ran a few minutes of the film to show them how much the copy was improved. It was remarkable! There would still need to be creative embellishments required before it could be shown commercially, of course, but the heart of the movie had been brought back to life! Robert had so intently watched it all the way through the first time, breaks and all, that he now noticed the many added bits Goodman had incorporated, using tiny strips that had been saved as they were dropped from the reel over the years.

Goodman's expensive invoice for the job was paid by check, and, considering the rush service, worth every penny in Robert's estimation.

Casey was still alert enough to watch Goodman place both the copy and original print in separate film cans, as Robert was effusive in his grateful farewell.

"You must be exhausted, and hungry," he suggested, as they made their way down the two flights of steep stairs to the street.

"I could use a nap." Casey agreed, "But hold up a minute. I've got to tie my shoelace."

She placed the can she was carrying on a convenient window ledge, and Robert placed his next to it, offering his arm to steady the girl as she bent down. Her mundane little exercise took only a few seconds, but it's amazing how much can happen in that short span of time.

Something rushed past, and both of them, after another couple of seconds, suddenly saw a young woman racing away with their two film cans!

Casey was the first to react. She jumped up and pursued the thief at an all-out sprint! Robert stood slack-jawed in disbelief as his agile partner tackled the girl about thirty yards down the sidewalk, and they sprawled clumsily intertwined as the cans rolled into the intersection! Cars were swerving to miss them!

Robert finally put himself into motion at that realization, but Casey was still more alert to the situation. She released her grip on the girl, and, bouncing back to her feet, darted into traffic to retrieve the cans before they could be smashed flat!

Robert arrived at the scene, shocked to discover he knew the miscreant, still sitting in a daze on the sidewalk!

"Why... Miss Bugnum!"

"Give me a hand, will you," she offered hers, and he naturally obliged. But once on her feet, she took off again without another word.

"Why didn't you hold her?" Casey complained. She was restrained by the film cans under each arm.

Robert shrugged. "Well, what would we do with her? Having her arrested would be as much of a nuisance for us as for her."

"How do you figure that?" Casey ignored the gawking people passing in each direction, most of which had witnessed some part of the brawl.

"We'd lose at least a whole day talking to the police, making a complaint, explaining everything, which would sound like a farce to them. Need I go on?"

"I guess you're right. And my uncle was right, as well. This film is more important than I thought up until now."

"You did great, Casey my girl," Robert patted her on the back.

Like an obedient dog, Casey thought.

"A worthy protector," he continued benevolently, "Which, frankly, I wouldn't have believed before this happened."

The blasé New Yorkers, most of them, had proceeded on their way, and the two of them began walking too, Robert taking the lead back to Facsimile Films.

"Well, thanks, Robert, old chap," she replied, with a full measure of sarcasm, "Now what do we do?"

They didn't concern themselves with Sasha once she was out of sight, but were aware now there were people who would do almost anything to possess the now more than mythical Matthews film.

'Let's go back and have Goodman wrap the original for shipping. I want to mail it back to Jessie right away."

Immediately after entering the front waiting room, Robert heard something coming from the back room that sounded vaguely and then precisely familiar. Goodman didn't hear them enter his workroom because the newly restored Matthews/Astaire film was running, at full volume, on a screen at the back of the room! Robert had to clap his hands together sharply to get his attention, and when that happened, the startled man almost fell off his stool. Robert's scowl was enough to convey his displeasure without trying to project his voice above the level of the scratchy soundtrack.

Goodman managed to stop the projector and began mumbling something that might have made sense if he'd taken the time to arrange his words more coherently, but Robert ignored it.

"How many prints did you make?" he demanded to know, and Goodman, drained of all duplicity, whispered "Only two."

"You had no right," Robert declared, like a judge who was about to pronounce a severe sentence. Would it be death by stoning or merely a hundred lashes with a bullwhip?

"I know," Goodman gasped.

As it turned out, the man's life was spared. All he had to do was rewind and remove the pirated print from the projector, then wrap the original, now only a pile of short lengths of film, and one new print, now that they had two, in a secure package. Robert retrieved his address book from his inside jacket pocket, and carefully addressed the package to Jessie's London home.

"I'm disappointed with you," Robert said, in a way completely opposite from the way they'd parted only a short while before.

"I just wanted a copy for myself." Goodman had finally found his voice, "I wasn't going to *sell* it or—"

"You'd better not have *another* copy hidden away!"

The man was shaking his head vigorously from side to side, as Casey left him with a final thought, "Shame on you," she said, as they closed the door and left him alone to mope.

Chapter 30

The passions of Dingle and Harleigh

Dingle Thimble was unusually cheerful, it seemed to his pal, Harleigh O'Halloran, as their tour bus weaved through the low hills along the edge of Los Angeles.

"You never even mentioned your daughter to me in all the years I've known you," Harleigh said, in a slightly accusatory tone, "And now you're acting like this will be the grand reunion of all time."

Dingle just grinned. Ever since Shlug's call, his anticipation had grown exponentially from zero to a billion brain blips. "Just because I didn't mention her doesn't mean I wasn't thinking about her. It was a cruel thing old Poundstack did to me, expelling me from my own country to keep me from the lass." He tapped Harleigh's knee sharply to add emphasis.

Both men were trying to memorize the route, which the promotional advertising promised would pass Fred Astaire's home, along with those of many other celebrities. Suddenly, as the bus buckled over a bump in the road, both realized they'd unfocused their attention.

Harleigh called out the next street sign, and Dingle quickly found it on the map in his lap.

"How could anyone force you to leave England?" Harleigh persisted, but Dingle had other things on his mind.

"Gawd blimey, it's a long story, and we'll have plenty of empty hours to go over it at length," the old codger grumbled, "Maybe tonight if you'll leave it alone now."

They would appear to be an odd couple, at first impression. Dingle, a runty Englishman with a red nose to rival Bozo the Clown's, and Harleigh, a tall African American who had spent the first twenty years of his life as the only child of the only black couple he knew who had emigrated to Ireland in the late '40's. It had not been an easy childhood for Harleigh, and he made the move to the United States as soon as he was of age. He kept his father's name, though, fully aware it was a fake one, and still respected his elders, in great part because of the hard road they'd chosen.

He was younger than Dingle, too, but they had two things in common that kept them together: horses and booze. By day they shared a fascination with the world of the racetrack, in all its complexity, and in the evening they shared their loneliness in drinking enough of whatever was available to blot out the monotony of their aimless existence.

The eminent arrival of Dingle's mysterious long lost daughter became in his mind the biggest event in his life since his daring elopement with Casey's mother, and their short marriage. Her death wasn't Dingle's fault, but her rich father blamed him anyway. Explaining all that to Harleigh could wait.

Despite his sarcasm, Harleigh was excited too, looking forward to meeting the girl Dingle called his little buttercup.

Chapter 31

Cock of the walk called Cook

L EW MURGIN'S OUTER OFFICE WAS treated like a lounge by a few of his on again/off again clients, who, though most of them were professionals, regular bit players in movies and TV, could still be impressed when a real celebrity came through the door.

The Goldcurls twins stopped arguing and old Ed Dobbins, a dependable walk through nonentity paused flipping through the trades when Elisha Cook, Jr. strutted in, snappily dressed and as bold as the barnyard's prize cock.

"Murgin called," he informed the agent's secretary, seated at her desk, trying to look busy.

"I'll tell him you're here," she rasped, reaching for the intercom button. One of the twins winked at Cook as he coolly surveyed the room. He didn't sit down, as if certain there would be no waiting for him.

Sure enough, the portal to his office opened wide, and Murgin, his dragon smile revealing both upper and lower fangs, ushered Cook inside.

"Have a cigar, Cookie," Murgin offered, as his client settled comfortably in a cushioned chair near the big desk in the center of the room. Cook helped himself to one, placing it in his suit's inside pocket. He didn't mind being called Cookie. Many people called him that, rather than Eli, which he didn't like at all.

"I was coming into the city today anyway." Cook explained with a little white lie, "so I thought I'd stop in to hear about the Astaire project."

Murgin made a face, which wasn't hard for him to do, since his every expression was a sight to see. "But, Cookie, I told you... It's not even a sure thing yet. I won't know for a week, at least."

"Well, you knew enough to call me. How solid do you think it is? Who's the director? Which studio is producing?"

"It's a special job, Cookie. More like an elaborate practical joke than a movie."

Elisha Cook Jr. could deliver a slow burn every bit as long as Jack Benny, and with more natural animosity, which is precisely what Murgin suffered until at last the veteran character actor spoke, obviously annoyed. "What do you mean, a practical joke? I'm a pro, Murgin. I don't do practical jokes."

His agent opened his mouth to speak, but since he hadn't yet formed a reply in his mind, Cook continued, just getting warmed up. "I've worked with the best. Bogart, Tracy, Mitchum... The best. And I can hold my own with anybody in the business, you know that."

"I know, Cookie, that's why I thought of you for this. You've got the chops to pull it off!"

Ignoring that flip flattery, the diminutive dynamo leaned forward upon Murgin's desk with a fullbore glare intended to intimidate, which would have been a wrap in one take on any set. "I've never worked with Astaire, so that would be something different. But if there aren't going to be any cameras around, I'm not interested."

"I understand, Cookie, I shouldn't have even mentioned it to you." Murgin's apologetic act was almost a match for Cook's, as if he really meant it. In fact, he did mean it. It was just so obviously insincere, it couldn't possibly be.

When the phone rang.

Cook reached for another cigar. This time he found a cigarette lighter and lit it.

"I'll call him back," Murgin barked to his secretary. She was answering the phone again, despite his explicit instructions. If she didn't work for minimum wage, he'd get rid of her. He hung up the phone and faced his sober-faced client.

"What's the bit?" Cook asked, curiosity trumping his pride.

"Astaire walks out of his house, carrying a movie reel. Maybe one of the others in his party is carrying the reel. You stick them up at gunpoint, take the reel, and make a getaway in your car."

Cook was trying to keep his temper tempered, but he had a naturally combative nature, and there was a foul smell surrounding this whole conversation. He leveled another slow stare in Murgin's direction, trying to decide if this whole episode was a practical joke. Was Allen Funt hiding in the closet with a camera?

"Everybody knows it's a gag except Astaire," he prompted.

"Well... no." Murgin shook his head.

"Astaire knows it's a gag, but nobody else does." Cook proposed another possible set-up, "Is that it?"

"No," Murgin muttered, trying to maintain a straight face because it was starting to sound like a weak Keaton two-reeler to him now, "Nobody knows it's a gag."

"You expect me to stick up a celebrity in broad daylight with no cameras on the scene, without any back-up of any kind?"

"You're the only man I know who could pull it off." Seems like he'd already made that comment, so it was obvious Murgin had exhausted his justifications.

Cook leaped at least a foot in the air, his face bright red, and from the outer office, everyone could hear him scream, "I'm not a gunzel, Murgin, I'm an actor! I can't believe you'd suggest such a thing to me!"

They all stopped chattering and turned their best ear toward the door, but an eerie silence pervaded both rooms.

Inside, Cookie was gagging and sputtering, having almost passed out, forgetting to take in any air as his fury overwhelmed him.

The phone rang again, and out of habit, Murgin picked it up. He took the call, from an assistant director at Warner Brothers. He listened for just a minute, then ended the conversation by saying "I'll call you back in five minutes."

Cradling the phone. He smiled broadly at Cook as if everything was suddenly alright, the entire eruption forgotten. He pulled a bottle of good whiskey and a glass from a drawer in his desk, "Have a drink, Cookie. There's a job for you right now, if you're up for it."

"Izzat so." Cook mumbled. But he did take the drink. His throat was hoarse.

"Warner's needs someone for a bit on the Rockford Files. Today. Right now."

"You're fired. I'm going to get a new agent."

"Well, if that's how you feel, I won't argue with you. I'll miss you, Cookie. We've been a good team for years."

"A team? That's ridiculous," he responded, unwilling to give the awful man any credit at all. Then, almost as if a thought made it to his lips without going through his brain first, "That's a pretty good series, that Rockford..."

"It's only one line, but you'll get double scale for the day because it's a rush job."

"One line? Not interested. I make it a rule never to take a role with less than three lines, which you should know by now."

"I know. But this is an emergency. Grady Sutton was lined up to be a bartender but he got the hives and his face is all splotchy with red spots, and that show's in color now..."

"Grady Sutton isn't right for a bartender anyway."

"They're shooting this afternoon, Cookie!"

"I won't do it unless I get at least three lines. I can do more with three lines than most guys can with three pages and a death scene. Otherwise, forget it."

The tiny actor with the maudlin mug appeared resolute, but didn't move from his chair except to retrieve his still lit cigar from the floor and puff it back to life.

Murgin instructed his secretary to get the man from the Rockford set back on the phone. He didn't waste time with any preliminaries when they were connected. "I've got Elisha Cook sitting here but he won't do the bit unless he gets three lines."

After listening for just a couple minutes, he said "I'll tell him", put down the phone and curtly informed Cook: "The writer isn't there, and they don't know if they can get ahold of him today."

"I'll write my own dialogue," Cook asserted, and Murgin so advised the man on the phone.

"What about Rockford's dialogue?" was the next question, to which Cook blithely replied, "I'll write Rockford's dialogue too." He hadn't been snoozing between scenes for the last thirty years. He had complete confidence in his abilities, not to mention an encyclopedic memory for melodramatic banter. Surprisingly, the deal was struck.

Murgin hung up the phone, a smug look of satisfaction on his face. He'd secured the promise of a bonus, or at least a favor in waiting, for supplying a pro of Cook's stature in a real pinch.

"Do you know where to go?" Murgin asked, only to get one last disdainful glance from Cook.

"Warner Brothers? I doubt if they've moved since last month. Of course I know where to go. I'll do this job, but I'll be looking for a new agent tomorrow, Murgin." He squashed his half smoked cigar in an ashtray with a sharp thump.

"I understand, Cookie."

His appearance betrayed nothing of the drama that had just transpired as the triumphant thespian tromped through the waiting room on his way out. Maybe he would look for a new agent, but more than likely, he wouldn't. Both of them knew Murgin's faults were slight compared to the average Hollywood ham huckster.

Chapter 32

One damn thing after another!

CASEY NOTICED ROBERT CHECKING THE rearview mirror in their car more than seemed necessary with the light traffic, and was about to ask why, when he quietly said, "We're being followed."

He didn't know it was Mosihing, Sasha and Asher, in their rented car, but as they passed a post office, he made a quick right, went all around the block, and swung into the parking lot of the imposing government building. He grabbed the wrapped film cans and ran inside, while Casey waited, warily scanning the streets in every direction.

Robert seemed securely satisfied with himself when he returned to the car. "See anybody suspicious?" he asked Casey.

"Lots of people look capable of anything, but nobody bothered me," she replied, smiling wanly. The tangle in the street with Sasha had put her on alert for the first time since they'd arrived in the states, and assorted bruises kept her in that state.

Robert got the car back into traffic as quickly as he could, certain their pursuers were still within sight, and would definitely be back on their trail. Debra wouldn't be expecting him, but that was the only place he knew to go that couldn't possibly be known to whoever was following them. He figured it was a 50/50 chance she'd be home to answer the bell.

He turned into a large commercial parking garage a few blocks from her apartment, grabbed the ticket from the machine at the gate, and drove to the rear of the building where, fortunately, there was an empty spot near a pedestrian exit. With Casey close behind, Robert rushed to the exit, then they scurried down an alley, up a quiet side street, and down another alley in the general direction they needed to go. Gasping for air in the shadows between two tall brick walls, they stopped to listen for signs of pursuit.

They stood there for several minutes, as motionless as a couple of department store mannequins, until finally Robert whispered, "I think we're okay."

Twenty minutes later, keeping to the shadows and dodging from tree to tree, they reached Debra's apartment building. It was a three story building. with perhaps two dozen apartments, each with a small balcony to give an illusion of open space. There was a genuinely spacious, well-manicured lawn in front, with a good-sized pool in the center. The pool was surrounded by dozens of lawn chairs, and the entire grounds were covered by tall shade trees. Many residents of all ages were enjoying the facilities and the natural pleasures of the warm sunny weather.

Debra, by herself, couldn't afford to live in such luxury, but fortunately for her, she had parents with enough financial largesse to subsidize her rent, thus providing private accommodations for their sole offspring, and peaceful, stress-free digs for themselves several miles away.

Casey knew little about Debra except for the occasional mentions by her usually taciturn traveling companion. According to Robert, Debra was beautiful, talented, sophisticated, cultured and remote. He never articulated 'remote directly, but Casey could envision that part of her personality between the few scenes he naively related in idle conversation.

Robert was relieved when the locked lobby door opened in response to his ringing her doorbell.

"Who is it?" Debra's voice came from behind her door on the third floor when Robert knocked.

"Robert Trabur," he announced loudly.

"Hmmm," Casey mused to herself. Not even his girlfriend calls him Bob.

Debra, barefoot and barely dressed in a polka dot bikini, opened the door and waved them in. Robert introduced Casey as Miss Thimble, without explaining their relationship, but Debra seemed to have little curiosity about her, another clue that Robert's dream girl didn't do much dreaming about him.

He was obviously momentarily transfixed by Debra's perfectly proportioned physiognomy, but Casey wasn't. Looking beyond their very casually dressed hostess, she was a bit surprised to see another person in the next room, sitting comfortably on a plush couch, smoking a cigar.

"I was expecting you," Debra said as she closed the door.

"You were?" Robert asked, absently.

"Yes. Your friend told me you were coming."

"My friend?" Robert asked, still unaware of the tubular gentleman rising to his feet, with a smirky smile on his face. He'd traded his cigar for a pistol.

"We're not really friends, Miss Lavish," the fellow said nonchalantly, "But I hope we can avoid being enemies."

"Oh dear," gasped Debra. It was her first sight of the gun too.

"Who the hell are you?" Robert demanded. It was an unusually hostile remark from him, but nobody took much notice of his newly macho posture.

Casey didn't know who he was, but she knew what he wanted. It was there in her arms, tight against her chest. Her thoughts racing, the only one that came to the forefront was flight. And the only place to flee was into the bathroom, it's door open between them and the corpulent, weapon-wielding menace beyond.

"All I want is that little package, my dear," the fellow addressed Casey, "I don't really want to shoot you unless I have to."

"You won't get away with this," Robert said, only because he thought he should say something. In a flash he realized this scoundrel had obviously phoned his office, Greta had given him Debra's phone number, and Debra had given him the precise directions to her apartment. Robert had led them most of the way, and here they were!

The two men exchanged a few more taunts, but Casey ignored them to throw a fleeting glance at Debra. "Follow me," she whispered, then grabbed the girl's hand to make sure she would.

Casey stepped forward, past Robert, as if she were about to hand over the package. Debra was close behind, and when they reached the bathroom door, both darted in. Casey slammed the door behind them!

Moishing heard the click of the lock, but he didn't let it bother him. "That door won't be any problem for my associate, young lady," he bellowed, much louder than was necessary.

"I don't want to harm you or your property, dearie," he spoke to the door, "so you might as well advise your visitor to hand over that package."

"Go away," Casey yelled, as if she expected him to dissolve into smoke and float out a window or vanish into thin air with a flash and a pop.

He took a few steps back to the phone, removed the cord, and yanked the other end out of the wall. Waving the pistol, as if to remind Robert that he was still in charge, his voice was again as soft and soothing as before Casey's expert dodge. "Out we go, Mr. Trabur. I'll follow you."

With her ear to the door, Casey heard them exit without closing the apartment door, and start down the stairs. Somebody else would be returning to bust down the bathroom door. Would the man with the gun come back too? Maybe he would, maybe not. Suddenly Casey conceived a desperate plan.

Sasha and Asher had watched Robert and Casey enter the building without being spotted themselves, as ordered, and then brought their car as close to the front entrance as possible, in case they would need to make a fast getaway. Neither of them had much experience driving, so maneuvering the short distance from where Moisting had parked it was a major undertaking in itself. The folks around the swimming pool were quite entertained by the spectacle, but Moisting's two inept subordinates were oblivious.

They didn't have long to wait before Trabur appeared, closely followed by Moisting, who had put the gun in his pocket, but still kept a tight grip on it. "3-B, third floor, up the stairs. Two girls in the locked bathroom," he whispered hoarsely to Asher. "Bring down the one with the package."

"How can I tell them apart?" Asher asked, never having seen Casey except a block away from where Sasha had wrestled her on the street.

"I don't need the one in the bikini, as charming as she is," the portly rascal hissed, his whisper a bit shrill, as he pushed his tall bully man to get him moving.

Robert had noticed the gun was holstered in Moisting's trouser pocket, and began to wonder how difficult it would be to take it away from him.

But he decided to keep that idea in reserve as Asher finally put himself in motion and disappeared inside the building. As soon as the would-be-except-he-was-such-a-pussy-cat villain was inside, and had deduced which was the bathroom door, he thumped on it a couple of times to determine how solid it was. As he suspected, it was hollow.

He positioned himself to keep his balance on one leg, then kicked the center of the door, which split it in half and sheared off the lock, so that it swung open without further action.

Both girls were standing in the tub. He caught sight of exposed flesh and shocked expressions, but ignored everything, looking for the film can. And there it was, sitting on the sink. He tested its heft, and, without a word, grabbed the rather sloppily dressed girl by the wrist. She hopped out of the tub, barefoot, but that escaped Asher's notice as he pulled her out into the hall and down the stairs.

Casey, scarcely covered by Debra's scanty bikini, grabbed the hidden towel-covered film reel and rushed to the balcony as soon as they'd started down the stairs. She only had a few seconds to escape before their trick was exposed. Moishing knew which girl was which, and it would only take a moment for him to find the cakes of soap and shampoo bottle in the film can!

She went to the balcony and was momentarily disheartened, not to mention terrified, to see how far it was to the ground. But there was another balcony below Debra's, and Casey had been the best gymnast of her college team, a skill she'd given up only because she enjoyed jockeying more.

Determining what she perceived to be the softest clump of bushes below, she dropped the stuffed towel, happy to see it didn't bounce after landing where she'd carefully pitched it.

It had been a couple of years since she'd attempted any gymnastic exercises at all, and there was no chance for any practice now, but she bravely went over the railing, hung by her hands from the bottom of the balcony like a monkey. and swung herself down, just inside the railing of the balcony below.

There was a loud thump when her feet hit the floor, and a second, softer thump when her bottom bottomed out. The elderly gentleman sitting in his easy chair, reading his newspaper, had a look of surprise on his face appropriate for this sudden appearance on his terrace, but Casey put him at ease by matter-of-factly proclaiming "Just taking a shortcut, Gov'nor."

She hitched up her bra, which had slipped below its purpose, and repeated the entire sequence, dropping more conveniently from the old fellow's balcony to the grassy lawn below.

After retrieving the reel, she considered her next move.

During Casey's athletic escape, Asher had delivered the girl and the empty film can to his co-conspirators waiting below just outside the front entrance. Robert laughed at Moisting's startled expression when they both recognized Debra. Quickly opening the film can, he threw it away in disgust, realizing he'd been outfoxed. Handing his weapon to Asher, the frantic Moisting and a slightly frazzled Sasha raced into the building and up the stairs.

Casey, with the reel loosely covered by the towel securely back in her grasp, raced around the back of the building, pulling up short at the corner to peep around to the front. Asher was holding a gun on Robert as they stood at the side of a car parked right in front of the building. Fortunately, Robert was facing in her direction, and while Asher's gaze turned toward the entrance, his quick thumb toward the pool was enough instruction to send her scampering in that direction.

Robert was getting a little steamed at this point. These characters were definitely out of order and he impulsively decided to do something about it. Without considering the consequences, he directed his fist at Asher's prominent chin. Although it was the first punch he'd thrown since a long ago high school brawl, it somehow connected, enough to knock the man off balance. Since the ungainly fellow was usually a little off balance anyway, this was not particularly noteworthy, but it was the bruising bump he got as he fell headfirst against the side of the car that knocked him unconscious.

Robert could hardly believe it, but Casey's insistent hissing brought him back to attention. She'd jumped in the pool after quickly sliding her precious package under a poolside lounge chair.

"Stay there," he mouthed without making a sound, well aware Moishing and the girl would appear at any moment, using hand motions to make his meaning clear. Then he raised the two fingers of his right hand to indicate he'd be back in two hours, and took off running at a dash as fast as he could go without giving her a chance to object.

Why is he giving me Churchill's victory sign, Casey wondered. She was impressed that he'd vanquished Asher, for the moment at least, but their battle was hardly won.

All of this had transpired in the few minutes it took the nefarious pair to reach Debra's apartment, search it, find Casey gone, and rush back out. Debra, forgotten in the frantic melee, had followed them back into the building, and they nearly ran her over on the stairs on their way back outside.

Chuck, wide-eyed and knock-kneed, opened the door of his apartment, saw Debra, and was about to ask what was going on, when she, in no mood for any explanation for him, put her fingers to her lips, and whispered "Shussh... It's a secret society initiation. I'll tell you about it later." and then hurried back to her apartment.

Some of the people in and around the pool observed parts of this activity, as well as normally private parts of Casey she was glad were now underwater, but apparently none of them had witnessed Robert's magnificent punch, and none of them had a clue about the seriousness of Casey's situation. If they wondered at all, they ascribed it to some kind of adult playtime.

Robert was scarcely out of sight when Mosihing and Sasha came running out of the building. Asher was coming around, rubbing his head, as they got to him.

"Where'd they go?" Moishing asked, but he didn't really expect a lucid answer.

"What happened?" Asher hadn't seen the fist coming, so he was completely bewildered.

"You get upstairs and keep that other female from getting to a phone," he ordered Asher, hoping the mug was alert enough to understand and obey. "You help him, Sasha...I've got to get to that bloke's car before they do!"

He jumped in their car and sped away, almost front-ended before he got 50 yards away because he forgot to proceed in the right side lane, the way traffic flowed in the United States.

He knew where Robert had parked his car, and was confident he could get there before Robert could on foot.

It was their last chance to get the film. Moisting had been so confident it would be a breeze to confiscate the goods without any complications, but nothing had gone as planned. Bringing Slinkring along was his biggest mistake. The man might look like Frankenstein's monster, but he was lurching along with the personality of a butterfly. And Sasha had foolishly put the couple on the alert with her misguided purse snatching attempt.

"I suppose you called the coppers," Sasha snarled at Debra when they got back up to her apartment. Debra was sitting next to her kitchen table, drinking what appeared to be a strongly mixed afternoon cocktail while munching on a plateful of carrots and celery. Even under stress, the girl was a calorie counter.

"Not yet, but I will. Look at that door! That will cost a lot to fix! And he damaged my phone connection too!"

Asher slumped on the couch, moaning a little, his hand holding his head, as if that would ease the pain.

"What's the matter with him?" Debra asked.

"Your Robert beat him up." Sasha replied, even though she hadn't seen the encounter,

"Robert... beat HIM up?!" Debra found that hard to believe. Asher had at first seemed to her a gigantic brute, and Robert was so... spindly.

Debra, uncharacteristically considerate, was reevaluating Asher. She put a towel under the hot water, and approached the now non-threatening giant, sadly sprawled on her cushions.

"Put this on your head," she offered, "Would you like an Advil?"

"What's an Advil," he asked, prepared to try anything that might help.

"A strong aspirin. It works pretty fast, usually."

There was some blood, but no current bleeding. Nothing too serious, Debra decided.

Sasha could barely conceal her contempt for both of them, but she held her tongue. Asher had always been a big doofus, and she had a natural dislike for this girl, someone like her, who was obviously self-absorbed, trading on her looks and sexuality. A competitor. She found the other overstuffed chair, plopped into it, and was soon examining her nails to be sure they hadn't been damaged in all the excitement.

After about an hour, Moisting came slouching in, his bravado evaporated, something like common sense having returned to take charge of his mental faculties.

Debra was no longer afraid of any of them. She confronted their leader before he had a chance to say a word. "What about my bathroom door? Look what your man did to my door!"

"I'll pay for your door. I'm not a bad guy, and neither are my... employees." He pulled his wallet out of his breast pocket and began laying out bills onto an end table next to a publicity photo of Debra in an all-white tennis outfit, holding a racket. Asher had been looking at that photo, and some of the others in the room, after he regained what senses he'd started the day with. His ardor for Sasha had dimmed over the past few days, witnessing her true self up close, but this American girl was rather fascinating to the big goofball.

"Here's a hundred dollars, Miss Lavish. That should get you a new door." Moisting was quickly reverting to his normally languid persona, plumb tuckered out after all that running up and down stairs, and his frustrated attempt at serious gangster play.

"We made a valiant effort, my friends, but this Trabur and Miss Thimble are more capable and resilient than I'd anticipated. I think our best course would be to return to England and try to intercept the package he sent to Jessie Matthews. It's surely another new print of the film. We can beat the mail by several days if we can catch a flight back right away."

"We're not even sure that package was addressed to Jessie," Sasha reminded him.

"I'm sure enough."

"Maybe he just returned her old pieced together print," Sasha scoffed.

"No," Moisting was physically whipped but still mentally strong. "He wouldn't have bothered to do that. What do you say, Asher? Have you had enough of this escapade?"

Asher made a gurgling sound from behind the towel he'd kept on his head on and off since Debra supplied it, but it couldn't be deciphered clearly as a yes or a no.

"But they still have another new print, don't they?" Debra wondered aloud.

What was it to her, Moishing wondered to himself. "He'll probably try to get to Astaire, and show it to him," he ventured, "That's what I'd do."

Debra was staring at Asher, who'd finally removed the towel, and was apparently at least following the conversation, if not quite ready to participate in it. Now that Debra had seen him in two very different settings, with at least two distinct expressions, a thought sprang to the forefront of her ever calculating mind. This man's terrible visage might be her key through an important Hollywood door.

"Are you feeling better now?" she asked in a purrlike whisper.

"I'm alright," he sat up straight, suddenly aware of his wimpish posture.

"Well, let's go then," Moisting got to his feet, giving Sasha a commanding jerk of his finger.

"I don't think he's fully recovered yet." Debra said, surprising herself as well as the others.

"He can sleep on the plane."

"I think he should stay here tonight." Oh, she was really feeling bold now!

Asher at his best wasn't quick in conversation, so with a headache factored in, and confused by the rapid turn of events, his silence wasn't unusual.

"Sasha and I are flying back to London tonight, Asher. Will you be joining us or not?" Moisting, having made his decision, was back to his normally imperious self.

Two people walked out of Debra's apartment a few minutes later, a fat man and his curvy girlfriend. Their overseas expedition was essentially over, but Asher Slinkring's American adventure was just beginning.

Chapter 33

Demure darling's daring escape

ASEY'S BODY HAD TURNED INTO an enormous prune. She'd been in the water up to her neck for over two hours, and dusk was falling. She'd seen Moisting and Sasha leave the building and drive away, but the gangling goliath with the face of a Halloween monster was still inside, so she dared not leave the pool for fear he'd spot her from a window overlooking the property.

Maybe Robert's two finger sign when he took off running meant two hours... so she tried to be patient. He would naturally be as wary as she was to have another encounter with any of the three villains they'd had to contend with.

Various apartment dwellers had come and gone since her momentous arrival at the pool, some a bit more curious than others. A couple of the single guys, more than a little impressed with the curvy dish in the tiny bikini, had tried to engage her in conversation. When her personality proved cooler than her hot façade, they ended up discussing her British accent, mostly, and she thought she'd convinced them she was visiting relatives.

She'd kept her eye on the towel-covered film nearby. Fortunately it remained dry, secured and undisturbed.

The light above the main entrance came on, and the last couple at the other end of the pool lazily dried themselves and made their way in that direction, when Robert finally showed up.

He was hardly indistinct, driving a brightly colored ice cream truck slowly through the grounds, a cheerful jingling tune announcing its arrival. It might have been comical except for the still precarious circumstances.

Robert spotted her simultaneously. He motioned her to come, and slowed to a stop a few yards past the front entrance.

Casey popped out of the pool, and her top again, which had shrunk even more in the water, hastily hitched the cups up over her nipples, and grabbed the film.

Robert missed the brief areola exposure, his gaze whirling left, right and backward for any sign of trouble, but he got the full impact of the nearly naked Casey running full tilt and bobbing bosoms to the truck. It was a stunning vision, but one he didn't have time to fully process. Then she landed inside, next to him, swinging the door shut with a loud slam.

He took off with a lurch and screech, ignoring the two youngsters who had dashed out of the building in response to the truck's seductive ice creamy melody. He drove too fast along the quiet neighborhood side streets until Casey let out a sharp "Slow down!"

Robert eased up on the gas and turned for a good look at his obviously embarrassed partner. She was trying to be as inconspicuous as she could, but there was too much of her to make that possible.

"That swimsuit is too small for you," Robert observed, without a hint of irony or humorous intent.

"No kidding!" Casey retorted, with every measure of sarcasm definitely intended. "It belongs to your skinny girlfriend!

Robert felt an unexpected rush of heat at the sight of her, but hastened to direct his attention back to the rearview mirror, relieved to see no headlights behind them. He made a turn, heading back to where he'd left the uniformed driver he'd bribed, having borrowed the man's truck for his rescue mission. But then, stealing another glance at Casey, he decided the girl didn't need the added humiliation of giving the ice cream driver an eyeful, and headed back to the alley behind the parking garage where their rented car was parked.

"How does it happen you're wearing Debra's bikini?" He had a momentary flashback of the girl opening the door to her apartment in that skimpy attire.

"I heard the guy with the gun say he was going to send someone else to bust down the door, so I figured—"

"You thought you'd confuse them by switching clothes…" Robert finished her explanation.

"Well, it worked." She didn't bother to explain how she'd reached the ground from the third floor without taking the stairs, and he didn't seem curious to find out.

As soon as they were in the darkened alley, Robert got out and took off his suit jacket. Casey accepted it with a simple "Thanks".

"Stay right here until I get back," he ordered her forcefully, "I have to return the truck. But it's not far."

She made no objection, feeling a little more proper, or at least considerably less naked with his coat around her.

Chapter 34

A dandy in drag, what a hoot!

Asher Slinkring was a pretty ugly man, but even more hideous as a woman. Dressed all in black, from nose to toes, with a wide black hat, gray wig and full veil, his face could be effectively hidden, his lanky, awkward body drawing most of the attention of innocent passersby. Debra too was in costume, her slim figure padded in many of the wrong places, a sack of potatoes look, with a wig of her own, dark glasses, and cheeks stuffed with cut-up handkerchiefs. They were completely transformed from the unlikely couple they'd been earlier in the day, who could have walked right past Robert and Casey in the airport concourse without being recognized. In fact, they did!

Casey was still clutching something wrapped in a towel close to her chest, wearing Robert's suit jacket. Her bare legs and feet more noticeable and out of place than the two costumed characters, even as foolish as they appeared. They were just entering one of the airport mall shops, a clothing store, when Debra saw them, too late to turn away from passing directly behind them. They were so focused on finding something for Casey to wear that they probably wouldn't have noticed a passing parade of kangaroos.

Arm in arm, Debra was leading Asher, who could scarcely see beyond the broad hat and veil. They found an electronic chart listing all the flights west that night, and decided an American Airlines nonstop flight to Los Angeles, departing in about two hours, would be the one Robert and Casey would most likely be taking.

She pulled out her father's credit card, the one he'd told her not to use unless it was a life or death situation, and purchased two tickets. She was confident they could accompany Robert and Casey on the same plane without being recognized, even if both couples were in the coach section.

Debra's acting experience was not very extensive, but she'd been dressing in costumes of every variety for years, and she'd spent an entire afternoon and evening devising her own and Asher's for this adventure. Poor Asher, still suffering from his headache, homesickness and general fatigue, allowed her to take command, Switching his allegiance from the overbearing Moisting, who he didn't like at all, to this spitfire of a girl, who smiled at him and made cryptic comments about his fascinating persona, whatever that was, hadn't been difficult at all. Having lived all his life as a horrible hulk, someone most people feared, this son of a Slinkring had never found it necessary to develop a pugnacious nature the way many short men do, trying to prove they're as tough as all those bigger louts. In fact, his self-confidence was so puny in relation to his appearance that he could be an easily manipulated personality, the perfect partner for Debra, whose self-confidence knew no bounds. She believed it was her natural inborn right to use and abuse anybody at all, certainly the lackluster Robert and mush monster Asher, and whoever else she might come across on her inevitable climb to stardom.

They hung back as unobtrusively as possible, considering their own appearance, as streams of travelers passed to and fro, then watched with full attention as a slightly rumpled Robert and freshly dressed Casey, in a pink sweater and gray slacks, made their way to the boarding area. Debra had decided to let them go first, and then find their own seats as cautiously as possible.

It was all Asher could do to keep himself all in one piece, balancing his hat and veil as best he could, mincing his steps delicately without stepping out in his normal gangling gait. The constricting skirt helped him concentrate on that part of his disguise.

Once again they passed right by Robert and Casey, who were stowing their carry-on luggage (though there wasn't much) and settling into their seats, as good as invisible in the crowded aisle.

Seated several rows behind the unsuspecting couple, Debra chuckled under her breath, nudging Asher with her elbow and favoring him with a wink. So far so good.

Chapter 35

From New York to Hollywood in one long leap

ROBERT SLEPT MOST OF THE way from New York to Los Angeles. Casey got in a few catnaps too, but only fitfully, unable to get comfortable enough to fully relax. They'd been fortunate to catch a nonstop flight within a short time after arriving at the airport, and there was no sign of pursuit from known or unknown tormentors. Despite their sense of security, however, the film can, still protected by Debra's bath towel, remained locked between Casey's legs throughout the entire trip.

Asher tried to sleep too, but midway between his first snore, Debra woke him with a sharp jab, and kept up a steady stream of dredged up subconscious meanderings about their fantasy futures in show biz. She wasn't tired at all, in a perpetual state of exultation at the amazing turn of fate that she'd been daydreaming about ever since her breasts bulged beautifully in her late teens, and the full length mirror behind her bathroom door told her she was a perfect B cup knockout with a svelte 24 inch waist and firm 34 inch butt circumference. Just one cup shy of Playboy playmate material, but exactly right to look great in fashionable clothes.

It's common knowledge that most female humans start out in those traumatic early years past childhood, entering puberty, with a negative appraisal of their own self-image, in comparison with all the other lovelies milling about in every direction. Some start out with a positive appraisal but soon come to a sober realization of just how they stand, in the middle of the pack, with enough charm to get by, but a few defects to be concealed as subtly as possible. Yet a few, like Debra, start out believing they're an immaculate princess, and hold that perception until their last queenly breath.

Asher, that wretched wreck, was exhausted, and kept nodding off, but his new master was relentless. She knew he was just barely believable as a female awake, but when asleep, sawing logs with his mouth open, his hat and veil askew, the masquerade obviously couldn't be maintained.

Chapter 36

A couple of amateurs on a stakeout

DINGLE THIMBLE CALLED THE TRACK early the next morning, to say he wouldn't be going in to work that day. He normally missed few days, and his work wasn't generally critical, so there wasn't a problem. Harleigh, who'd slept on Dingle's couch so they could get an early start, made a similar call to his office, but had to lie, saying he was sick, very sick, because his accounting duties were critical, and they'd have to hustle to find a replacement for the day.

Harleigh hadn't seen any of his family for decades either, so he realized why his pal Dingle was so excited about the possibility of seeing his daughter Cassandra, and just had to tag along. Losing a day's salary was the least of his concerns.

Together they'd taken the bus tour of the stars homes, noting in particular the address of Fred Astaire's grand estate, marking the route so they could find their way back to it in Harleigh's old Chevy. Harleigh, an unbiased onlooker, figured Dingle's chances of actually meeting his daughter were about 50/50 at the most optimistic, but Dingle of course figured it was a hundred percent certainty.

They stopped enroute for a quick breakfast, but by 9 AM they were parked a short distance from the gate to Astaire's home, as far to the outer edge of the shoulder of the road as they could manage, hoping not to attract too much attention in the exclusive neighborhood.

Dingle had come prepared, with his heavy-duty long distance binoculars, and was sure he'd be able to spot any young woman passing through that gate. Harleigh had come prepared, as well, reaching under his seat to pull out a full bottle of Imperial whiskey.

"It's Canadian Club's economy brand, you know," he assured his suddenly thirsty companion, "Not quite as smooth, but just as potent."

They settled in for what might be a long wait.

Chapter 37

On their way to meet The Man

THE FIRST THING ROBERT DID upon arriving in Los Angeles was call James Ames, Fred Astaire's agent, as they'd arranged previously, to schedule their meeting. Told to stay in place for a return call, Robert stood on guard at the pay phone for the long quarter hour before it rang. Since there were a dozen booths in a row, It wasn't too difficult to keep his clear.

Casey wandered about, but not too far, examining the quaint advertising posters and odd cultural artifacts of the enormous American airport. They seem to like *everything* big in this country, she mused.

He was beaming after the second brief call, as Casey joined him.

"Mr. Astaire is sending a limousine for us, Miss Thimble," he was floating a few inches above the ground, "It will be here in less than an hour."

Finally, things were looking up. Not having eaten anything at all for more than 24 hours, they looked for the nearest restaurant, and found a full service coffee shop no more than 100 steps away. Casey was amused at the novelty names for the amazing variety of breakfast combinations.

"I don't think her majesty, the Queen of England has this many options on her morning menu," she laughed, and Robert thought that was worth a chuckle too. This was the first time they were able to relax and share a joke since their journey began, or at least that's how it seemed, apparently to both of them. After ordering, Robert found himself staring at Casey's bust, picturing her as she was when she'd plopped herself in the front seat of the ice cream truck, her bulging bosom barely covered by Debra's too teeny bikini bra. There was no doubt the girl had a very curvy, sexy shape, though she didn't flaunt it the way Sasha did, for example. She kept her clothes loose and full around the waist on purpose, to deemphasize her hourglass figure. Something unusual was happening below his belt. He realized he had a full erection, and felt his cheeks redden in embarrassment.

Casey, between mouthfuls of the most delicious scrambled eggs she'd ever tasted, took a long look at Robert. Her first impression had been that he was a skinny middle-aged nerd, with about as much manly magnetism as a turnip, but she'd been surprised by his sturdy, studly leadership and particularly his surprising ability to knock Moisting's giant brute unconscious. Now that was really something! He caught her gaze, and she noticed his cheeks turning red. That was odd, she thought, and it subtracted a bit from his masterful image in her imagination, but at least he wasn't a pansy when a situation called for action.

After their meal, they just had time to buy some antacids, a large notebook and a fat black marker in a nearby shop before making their way to the cab stand where the limousine was soon to arrive. Robert was to hold a sign saying *Astaire' in large letters. The rest of the notebook would come in handy if any addresses or other information needed to be transcribed at the meeting.

Feeling warm and satisfied, neither of them had the least suspicion that two sneaky schemers were following them every step of the way, still dressed as before in their ridiculous costumes. Asher was feeling almost natural now, except for the veil. He was suitably restrained, in character in his first role, encouraged by the frequent compliments and occasional butt pats from his cunningly charming accomplice.

When Debra saw Robert and Casey climb into Astaire's limousine, she grabbed Asher's arm and hustled him into the first cab in line, patiently waiting for a fare.

"Follow that limousine," she commanded the driver in her most strident tone.

"Oh, goody", he replied softly, adding, without expressing it out loud, 'a chase'. Then, after checking out his oddly dressed passengers, 'Maybe an all-out Hollywood adventure!' A 20-year-old aspiring comedian, he'd started driving a cab as his day job, certain he'd eventually be carrying some important producer or director or agent who would be able to start him on his show biz career.

"Did your husbands get away from you girls?" It was just his nature to be glib with whoever stepped inside his cab, and these two silly looking old bags didn't intimidate him any more than a half dozen gangsters would.

"Just watch the road," Debra snapped, "Don't lose that car!" Her words were a little garbled because she still had some of the padding in her cheeks.

"I won't lose it. But I do hope there won't be any gunplay when you catch them... I'm sensitive when it comes to violence."

"You're a motor mouth, aren't you. A big fat motor mouth." Debra saw his enormous chin and naturally assumed the rest of him was proportional.

"No, I'm just a skinny little motor mouth, actually. Where is that limousine going, do you have any clue?"

"Just don't lose him."

"Are you ladies from out of town?"

Debra didn't bother to answer the question, and Asher didn't bother either.

"I'm not only a cab driver, I'm a private investigator too," he babbled on, "If you've got a problem, I might be able to help."

"Well, we're with the FBI, so you'd better mind your own business," Debra said with as much authority as she could muster.

He laughed, as much at her snippy tone as her comeback, but held his tongue. They drove on, following the limousine to the Beverly Hills exit, and on along the winding road to that affluent suburb. Finally he couldn't resist attempting further conversation with the mysterious FBI agent with the cheap wig and flamboyant hat who hadn't yet uttered a word.

"That's a nice veil you're wearing. You don't see a lot of veils anymore. If you're in mourning. I'll drop the subject."

The car ahead was proceeding at a leisurely speed, so he didn't have any trouble keeping it in sight, no more than one car ahead as they went along the broad boulevard. They were on a tree-lined road now, out of the crowded downtown LA traffic. By this time, just from the brief views of his passengers, he was pretty sure the person behind the veil wasn't in mourning. His beard was the giveaway. Asher hadn't shaved in three days, and it showed.

"If I can guess why you're chasing that limousine, will you give me a more generous tip than otherwise?" He'd get something out of them one way or another.

"You'll be lucky to get a dime if you don't shut up," Debra warned him, but she forgot to use an old lady voice, and since she'd just taken the last of her handkerchiefs out of her mouth, the cabbie could tell she was younger than her padded dress and gray wig tried to portray her.

"Come on, sister, what's your game? You're not fooling anybody in that get-up. You're an amateur, and your mother's mustache needs a trim."

Asher put up his hand to squelch Debra, leaned forward so his mouth was only a couple of inches from the cabbie's ear, and whispered a husky threat. "Here's your tip in advance. Shut up or this is your last ride." He was only a pussycat, but his growl was sonorous enough to make anybody quake. The rest of the trip proceeded in silence.

Chapter 38

Everyone meets at Fred's place

"That's odd", their driver mused, as the limousine slowed, approaching Fred Astaire's gated estate, "That car was parked there when I left this morning." It was an older car, rather beat-up, definitely out of place in this upscale neighborhood. Not a single home sat on less than an acre of well-manicured lawn and grounds.

Robert could see there were two men sitting in the front seat, with no evidence of any attempt to be on their way. "I wonder if—" he began, but Casey nudged him and gave him a subtle shake of her head. No need to alarm the driver, she instinctively decided. Besides, there was another unexpected distraction just outside the locked gate at Astaire's fashionable address. Two young women were standing there, inappropriately attired for this early morning hour in low-cut, ankle-length silk evening gowns and high heels, both extending their thumbs in traditional hitchhiking poses. They were both blondes, as alike as sisters, attractive in a brassy way (at least in Casey's immediate appraisal), but who, aside from their glamorous facades, seemed rather droopy and forlorn.

The driver pulled up, got out, and made his way to the intercom. "Car trouble?" he inquired, idly.

"We were at a party up the road, but it got too rowdy, so we left."

"Oh." He was well aware there were loud, crude, vulgar and worse such gatherings behind the walls of some of the grand mansions in the neighborhood. The young ladies were dressed for such occasions, in their slinky finery, so their story seemed logical. They must have made their exit about dawn.

Astaire's mother answered his call to the house.

"I've got the couple Mr. Astaire was expecting, madam," he reported in his most professional manner. In private he called Mr. Astaire Freddie, and his mother Flossie, her nickname for Florence.

"I'll buzz you in," she replied.

"Good luck," he said to the girls, as he got back behind the wheel. They drove inside, the gate swinging closed again behind them. It was a circular driveway in front of the three story house, with an attached three car garage on one side, and another smaller building of indeterminate use, probably a gardener's shed or enclosed garden, on the opposite side. There were extended balconies on the top floor, and it had the appearance of a most comfortable home in every particular.

Robert and Casey were escorted directly through the front entrance by the driver, who, without a word, opened a closet door in the entrance hall and hung his chauffer's cap on a hook inside.

He then led them into a large room, like a high-ceilinged grand hall, that had paintings and tapestries adorning the walls, plenty of what looked like miniature statues and books in glass encased cabinets, but no furniture to sit on. A broad staircase led upstairs, and upon them, bounding down in a graceful lope, came Fred Astaire himself. There was a wide smile on his face, and a hand extended as he bounced off the final step.

"Hello," he said simply, but Robert, to his own surprise, was unable to utter a word. He was awestruck, observing the man's entrance like something out of one of his movies.

Casey, more impressed with horses than people, was not particularly excited by this middle-aged man dressed in loose lounge trousers which were secured around the waist by what looked like a scarf, an ordinary golf shirt, and slippers.

"An honor to meet you, sir," she said anyhow, having been advised, of course, that this homely old fellow was an important person.

And then Robert, the spell broken by her words, managed to say "I'm Robert Trabur, and this is my associate, Miss Thimble." He was carrying his notebook in one hand, and Casey was carrying her thick red towel under her arm, like a big purse.

"There's some unusual activity on the street, sir," the driver interrupted. He was still standing by, off to the side, as motionless as a statue. More like a butler than a limousine driver, if such a distinction could really be made.

"Unusual?" Astaire came to attention, knowing his man's understatements often hid far more serious issues than simply 'unusual'.

"There was a suspicious looking car parked about a block away, right on the side of the road, when I left for the airport this morning, and it's still there. Shall I call the police?"

His master thought about it for at least two seconds. "No, I don't think so. The first patrol car that spots it will find out why it's there."

"And there are two hitchhikers right outside the gate. Two young ladies. They claim they escaped a disorderly party..."

Astaire grimaced. It wasn't an expression ever caught on film, and for good reason. He looked okay with a smile on his face, but in real life, the more normal contortions of his natural features, the cracks and creases of an ordinary face, weren't flattering at all.

"What do you expect me to do?" There was more than a trace of annoyance in his voice.

His chauffer was unruffled. "It occurs to me I'll be taking these folks back to the city, and, with your permission, could give the girls a lift too,"

Astaire gave him a blank look, then blurted "Go ask my mother." It seemed a rather queer utterance from a man with the demeanor of a grandfather, but the chauffer bowed ever so slightly, turned and disappeared up the stairs.

"That chauffer of yours acts more like a butler than a driver," Robert said, with a chuckle, "In fact he's a dead ringer for an old actor named Arthur Treacher."

Astaire's smile had evaporated, but his neutral expression didn't betray any emotion, positive or negative.

"He is my butler, and my driver as well. And he is Arthur Treacher. I hired him after his acting career had run its course. Please don't embarrass him by mentioning his previous career. It's the only touchy subject he'd prefer not to discuss."

Chapter 39

What's Jay Leno doing here?

It looked like an estate sale must have been going on at the entrance to Fred Astaire's home when the cab carrying Asher and Debra approached the scene. The limousine they'd been following had just pulled up to the gate, a couple of overdressed women were standing nearby, and another car was parked just up the road.

Debra thought fast, improvising was her talent. "there's our contact... that car up the road. You can let us out there."

Their moose-jawed cabbie couldn't figure it out but he knew there was something very peculiar going on. He resisted the impulse to heckle his passengers anymore, though, and accepted the bills Debra put in his hand with a fully forced smile and a final "Have a nice shoot-out."

"Keep the change," Debra said, ignoring the taunt. The cash amounted to twenty cents more than the charge shown on the meter.

After his passengers had exited, the cabbie pulled ahead several yards, found a place wide enough to make a U turn, and came back toward Astaire's gate slowly, trying to see if the occupants of the parked car were also wearing ridiculous costumes. Debra and Asher were still standing outside the car, and appeared to be engaged in an intense conversation with the man in the driver's seat.

The limousine, by this time, had passed through the gate, but the two young women were still standing at the side of the road. He pulled up and called out "Need a cab?"

Crystal gave him her snootiest look, and said "No thanks."

"Are you sure?" he persisted.

"No thanks", April smiled. She didn't give men snooty looks without provocation.

"I know you girls!" the cabbie exclaimed. He had a memory for faces, and these two had faces worth remembering. "You're the Goldcurls!"

They were surprised. Pretty girls were common in these parts, and they were seldom recognized outside their usual haunts.

"We were on the same bill just a couple weeks ago. The Tickle Me club."

Crystal gave him a good look, and realized he did look familiar.

"You remember me, don't you?" He showed her his profile, "The chin."

"I remember you," she groaned, "You tell stale jokes."

"Well, that's your opinion, but I've been getting more gigs all the time. Pretty soon the name Jay Leno will mean something."

"Dream on, cabbie."

"What are you girls doing here? Are you part of the act today, whatever it is?"

"It's none of your business, but we might need a cab a little later. How about checking back in about twenty minutes?"

"Time is money, sweetheart. I can't dawdle around here on the possibility you might need a cab..."

"Okay, get lost then." Crystal dismissed him.

April admired her partner, who was never at a loss for words. She had nerve herself, but wasn't as swift with the comebacks.

"See you around," Leno called out cheerfully, as he pulled away.

But he was getting more curious by the minute. He should have headed straight back to the city and concentrated on making some money, but this set-up was just too intriguing to ignore. He drove away in low gear, looking for a side road or long driveway in which he could park and keep a watch on the goofy characters surrounding Fred Astaire's estate. He found one, the tree-lined driveway to Jimmy Stewart's place, across the road, only a quarter mile away. He happened to know Stewart was out of town, on location in Santa Fe, New Mexico, making a movie called The Cheyenne Social Club. He'd read it in Variety the day before. He figured he could sit there all day without being bothered if he wanted to. He parked, pulled out his binoculars from the glove compartment, and found a comfortable spot to sit in the crotch of a leafy tree.

Chapter 40

Astaire, the surpriser, gets a surprise

J UST AS ROBERT WAS BEGINNING to wonder if their host's hospitality would extend to a more comfortable setting to discuss their
business than standing in his formal trophy room, a phone nearby
began ringing. Two rings only.

That might be for me," Astaire muttered, raising a finger to
indicate there would be a slight intermission.

Arthur, having obviously answered a phone upstairs, was returning back down the stairs. Robert noticed he was now wearing a formal black jacket with tails. "It's her again, sir," he said, when his own
were able to meet his employer's eyes.

"I was afraid of that," Astaire mumbled once more, which
appeared to be a habit.

"Hello darling," he chirped into the receiver when he picked up
the phone on a table nearby.

"Oh yes, you know it," he went on, and then there were a few
more assurances and a few more 'darlings' and a couple of 'dear's
before he could get off. Shaking his head absently, apparently still
thinking about the caller, whoever she was, Astaire guided them with
an outstretched hand into an adjacent room, a smaller room with

floor to ceiling book shelves filling two walls, comfortable chairs and a twenty foot long couch in the form of a half circle. There was also a good-sized table surrounded by straight back chairs, and upon two of them sat two serious looking gentlemen in black suits, white shirts and black ties, who nodded when introduced, but didn't make any effort to stand or offer a handshake.

They looked like professional pallbearers.

Astaire's introductions were as somber as their expressions.

"Mr. Ames, my agent, Mr. Robbins, my lawyer. Miss Trimble and Mr. Traitor"

"That's Thimble," Casey corrected him.

"Oh yes, Thimble. An unusual name," Astaire held a chair gallantly for her, and they were all seated.

"And my name's Trabur," Robert added, "It's a pleasure to meet you gentlemen."

From this room, they could hear a piano being played somewhere else in the house. Played badly, with closely repetitious passages, and many long pauses. A youngster getting lessons perhaps?

Mr. Ames cut right to the business at hand, without offering additional pleasantries, "We've done a little research on Jessie Matthews, Mr. Trabur, but Mr. Astaire hasn't had any contact with her for over 30, almost 40 years."

"I know, but it's their contact in 1932 that brings us here."

"To what are you referring, exactly," Mr. Robbins was using his coolest lawyerly tone, which both Robert and Casey couldn't help noticing, along with the equally frigid expression of Mr. Ames and the tentative manner and furrowed brow of Mr. Astaire.

Robert addressed Astaire directly, "Do you remember the movie you made with Miss Matthews in 1932, during your vacation in London?"

He looked positively blank for a moment, and then a pastel memory clicked in, soft at the center, fading at the edges.

"I didn't make a movie with Jessie Matthews. I couldn't have, even if I wanted to. I was under exclusive contract with Republic Pictures then."

"Well, it wasn't ever released..." Robert tried a hint, well aware the man had experienced more over his lifetime than any random dozen ordinary people, patient for a decades old day or two casual interlude between major films to be accessed from the tangle of his memories.

"Oh, well, they shot some home movies of us, as I recall, just for kicks, on her movie set. What about it?"

"Well, it might have been inconsequential to you, Mr. Astaire," Robert was warming to his soon-to-come revelation, "But after you returned to the states, they added a lot to it, and made a full length movie using that footage."

He was trying to throw in enough movie terms to show them he knew what he was talking about. But that was of no concern to these three serious characters. All of them were momentarily speechless. But lawyers aren't speechless for long.

Mr. Robbins said "You mentioned something about a great deal of money on the telephone with Mr. Ames..." It was certainly a question, even without the question mark.

"I'm not an expert about the distribution of things like this, but it seems to me it could mean a great deal of money for Miss Matthews,.." Robert was beginning to understand their cautious attitudes, "And for Mr. Astaire too, of course."

The agent was the first to pick up on that remark, "Money *for* Mr. Astaire?" He wanted assurance he'd heard it correctly.

"Of course," said Robert, "Miss Matthews insisted nothing could be done without Mr. Astaire's permission and cooperation."

The three of them exchanged glances and expressions simultaneously, Casey noticed, and expended simultaneous sighs of relief.

"Frankly, Mr. Trabur," the lawyer looked entirely different with a smile on his face, "Based on your initial conversation with Mr. Ames, we were expecting some kind of shakedown."

"I thought you were going to tell me I had a middle-aged son I never knew about," Astaire burbled, with a kind of snorting laugh.

"Oh, I'm sorry," Robert was truly apologetic, "I should have been more clear about—"

"We jumped to unwarranted conclusions, I'm afraid," Ames interrupted, "It's the times we're living in. Everybody's got some kind of scheme in mind, it seems sometimes."

Fred Astaire didn't appear to be as reassured as the others. "I'd like to see what you're talking about," he said firmly.

At that, Casey gently pulled the reel of film from her towel, and held it up for all to see.

Chapter 41

The gaudy Goldcurls Twins

Mrs. Austerlitz not only okayed Arthur's suggestion to offer the two young hitchhikers a ride, she told him to bring them in to wait in comfort. Flossie was a kindly old gal, and just a little lonely. Loving son Fred provided her every need, but didn't spend much time with her. If it weren't for Arthur, she might not see anyone for days at a time.

She met them at a side door, the door into the garage, so they wouldn't disturb her son's visitors, and saw immediately that both girls' gowns were damaged, ripped and dirty, and they obviously needed makeup repair after several hours out in the sun dodging dust and detritus from passing cars. By the time they'd ascended the two flights of backstairs to Flossie's domain on the top floor of the house, the three women were acting like long lost friends, fast friends indeed.

They introduced themselves by their real names, Crystal Witzenburg and April Falstaff, without mentioning their stage name, the two and only Goldcurls Twins.

Someone was playing a piano, badly, elsewhere in the house, but Flossie didn't mention it, so they tried to ignore it. If that was the master of the house, he obviously wasn't as talented in every area of show business as he was as a dancer.

"Do you know how to play pinochle?" she asked, after the girls had touched up their faces and adjusted their fragile dresses as best they could. They were sitting out on the balcony, her favorite place whenever the weather permitted, and it usually did.

"I don't think I ever played pinochle." Crystal demurred with a sweet smile, and April shook her head.

"Oh, it's fun. I'll teach you. Those people downstairs with my son might be here for hours."

It didn't fit into their plans, but there didn't seem to be any alternative for now. At least they were in the house, which was the biggest hurtle, and they could barely hear that awful piano from the balcony.

Chapter 42

Songwriter with impressive resume

ARTHUR HAD BROUGHT IN A tray with a pitcher of iced tea with several tumblers. Robert was feeling a lot more comfortable, and Casey seemed to be at ease too. Thankfully, the piano was no longer in operation. It had been an irritant.

The door opened and a tiny elderly man leaned in, pausing until Astaire turned in his direction.

"I'm going home, Fred. I'll see you later."

"Oh, Irving, stick around. We're going to run an old movie. A musical. You might find it amusing."

"Who wrote the music?"

"Noel Coward." Robert had supplied a few of the most significant facts about the film, enough, he hoped, to convince this elite audience that it was a professional production.

"I can write better songs than Noel Coward," the old fellow said dryly. "I'll see you later." He closed the door and was gone.

Robert chuckled, just short of a guffaw. "Your friend thinks he can write better songs than Noel Coward! That's rich!"

"Well, actually, he can, "Astaire drawled, "Let's see... Cheek to Cheek, Change Partners, Always, Blue Skies, White Christmas..."

Robert gasped. "That... little guy... is Irving Berlin?"

"Yeah," Astaire laughed at Robert's goofy expression, "I know. He's not very imposing in person. All of us living legends have a hard time living up to our reputations."

"I'm sorry if I—"

"Forget it," Astaire cut him off from delivering a lame apology. "Let's see this rare little movie." He wouldn't admit it, but he was curious to see what Robert obviously considered so important. "Gene Kelly has a projection room right in his house. Arthur, see if you can get Kelly on the phone. And then find a film can for this reel. You know where they are. Use one of the TV cans if there aren't any empties."

Arthur dialed the number from memory, and waited for someone to pick up.

"Kelly only lives a few miles from here... if he's home."

"I have to be in court this afternoon, Fred," Mr. Robbins said, "I don't think you'll need me any more today."

"Of course, Chuck. Thanks for coming on such short notice." Astaire was ever the gentleman, even apart from his screen personality.

Chapter 43

Trespassers alert the old lady

FLOSSIE HAD PERSUADED THE GOLDCURLS girls to join her at pinochle, but they were a bit slow catching on, it seemed to her. Her gaze wandered to the broad lawn below, and she caught sight of something moving in the bushes near the fence. Something that appeared to be a human being, a very weird appearing human being dressed in an outlandish costume, closely followed by a second peculiar person, and both were in full sneaking postures, moving straight toward the house!

"Trespassers!" she exclaimed, jumping to her feet with remarkable vigor for her age, and then rushed inside to her phone. Crystal and April scanned the grounds, and they, too spotted the interlopers. Debra and Asher hadn't lifted their gaze above the ground floor, neither of them experienced as housebreakers. They'd circled the house from outside the fence and chosen a backside route that appeared to face the fewest windows and doors. The ladies three stories above were barely visible from below, only their heads showing above the balcony walls.

Asher covered the distance from the fence to the wall of the house in a few scant seconds, and Debra wasn't far behind. On his knees, he poked his head up to peer inside a window, and there was Arthur on the other side of the room, having just removed the reel of a TV drama that his employer had appeared in a few years earlier from its case, and placed the new old Jessie Matthews film in its place. The window was open, and Asher heard Flossie's loud "Arthur! Come at once!" from somewhere else in the house. Asher didn't connect her urgent command with his own presence because his attention was focused on Debra's bright red towel, the towel they'd been trailing all the way across the country! When Arthur dropped everything and hurried out of the room, Asher threw the window wide open and awkwardly scrambled through it. In moments the naked reel and the red towel were in his grasp, and he handed them out to Debra before escaping himself. They raced without a word back out to the perimeter of the property and the concealment of the bushes and trees there.

Chapter 44

Leno hangs around

JAY LENO, THE CABBIE WITH the silly name, was bored. Southern California was definitely worth a visit, even a yearlong sort of sabbatical from the usual eastern seaboard plethora of nightclubs, his normal habitats, but a native New Yorker like Leno was used to bustling streets, noise and action. Plenty went on behind locked doors and high walls out here in LaLa Land, everyone on the make, primarily in some area of show business, but out in the open, it was all pastureland. Astaire's estate, for example, surrounded today by little pockets of petty plots, was itself as sedate and calm as a secluded private park that had been closed for the season.

He decided to check out the car parked up ahead on the shoulder, having been there, apparently, for hours. Leaving his cab safely hidden where it was, he hiked the few hundred yards to the well-worn Chevy.

Harleigh and Dingle were pleasantly inebriated, and made little attempt to hide the now almost empty bottle of rye whiskey they'd been sipping for hours as Leno approached on foot.

"Morning, gents," He sang out, amiably. Waiting for somebody?"

"Tha's right," Dingle replied. There was nothing wrong with that, so he didn't mind admitting it to this inquisitive stranger.

"We're waiting for shomebody." Harleigh added, though it was unnecessary.

"Those two characters I saw you talking with earlier?"

"Who?" said Dingle. He'd completely forgotten them.

"Those two in costume. The tall guy with the hat and the gal with the padded dress."

"Oh, thoshe two," said Harleigh, slurring his speech just a little, "We're not waiting... for them."

"I'm waitin' for my dotter Casey," Dingle's speech was normally slurred in a lowdown Cockney accent, so his drunken speech was almost identical.

"Wutch its to you?" Harleigh spoke up, a little combative, in his chips.

"I'm waiting for someone too," Leno was clever at promoting conversation with strangers. He'd been studying Allen Funt on Candid Camera for years. "Maybe we're waiting for the same person."

"No," said Dingle, and that seemed to be the end of it.

"What's your daughter's business with Fred Astaire? Is she a dancer." Leno could take rejection without missing a beat. Bombing regularly in clubs with bad jokes had given him a tough hide for someone of his tender years.

"Whoo ur yu anysway?" Harleigh gave the young man a very haughty look, which didn't register any more than his combative speech.

"I'm Jay Leno. I'm a comedian. Temporarily a cab driver."

"yur not verry *funny*."

"I'm going to be a top comedian someday. On television, like Bob Hope."

Harleigh snorted involuntarily. "With *that* faze!" he had lost every bit of his normal diplomacy. "You haven gota chanze."

"How about Jimmy Durante," Leno countered. He enjoyed arguments with drunks. It reminded him of home. "Jimmy Durante is funnier looking than I am, and he's a big star."

"Heesh funnier looking, but he's alsho *funny*!" Harleigh had him there, or at least he thought he did.

"My dotter has a valable film for Mishtar Asteer," Dingle interjected from left field.

But that's all Leno could get out of them, because far down the boulevard he first heard, then saw a patrol car approaching with its siren blaring and top light spinning. He jumped off the road and was confident he hadn't been seen at all because the police were coming from the opposite side of the car from where he'd been standing. By the time they came to a stop next to the old Chevy, he was many yards off the road, behind the trees, heading back in the direction of his cab.

Chapter 45

Arthur Treacher has a bit

A RTHUR, CARRYING THE FRESHLY PACKED film case, entered the study calmly to inform his master that "We've spotted a couple of trespassers, sir. The police have been alerted."

"I thought I heard mother calling you about something. It happens," he reassured his guests, "A nuisance, but usually not very serious."

"You really should install some better security, Fred," Ames asserted, remembering a few other occasions.

Astaire ignored the comment with a shrug. "We'll go on over to Kelly's place as soon as the police get here," he declared emphatically.

"I wonder if I might come along, sir?" Arthur asked in his most humble tone. "I was a fellow player with Miss Matthews in those long ago days." He didn't look very alert, but he hadn't missed any of their conversation, either in or out of the room.

It was an unusual request from the usually taciturn Treacher, but Astaire said "Of course," without hesitating for a second.

"I never knew that, Arthur. Were you in any of her movies?"

"On the stage, sir. I actually sang a duet with her. But I doubt if she'd remember. It wasn't a very good play, and it closed after only a few performances. Six weeks altogether, as I recall,"

"You sang a song? Arthur, you continue to amaze me," Astaire mused, sincerely impressed. "Was it a good song?"

"Are you mocking me, sir?" Butlers, even imitation butlers, take offense easily.

"Mocking you?! Certainly not. I've always considered you a fellow professional."

They were ignoring the others, at least one of whom followed their conversation in rapt attention as if it were critical dialogue exchange from a classic movie.

Arthur continued his reminiscence, dredging up details he hadn't thought about at all for decades, even though he probably had no more than a fleeting memory of them at all.

"It was the title song of the musical, 'Hold my Hand', though I don't recall the name of the composer. Produced in the fall of 1931 at the Gaiety Theater in London."

"The Gaiety?" Astaire was suddenly animated, as if a battery had suddenly switched on. "I played the Gaiety when I was a teenager! With my sister!"

"I should have known you'd trump me, sir," Arthur observed dryly.

Astaire laughed. "Of course you must join our party, Arthur. My memories of Jessie Matthews are pretty hazy, and I might need yours to help sort them out."

"And there's another matter, sir, about the two young ladies. Perhaps I should call a cab for them."

"Oh yes, the party girls," Fred frowned. All of the expressions on that craggy countenace were broader than those of most people.

Flossie followed them down the stairs when they were summoned.

"Where are the police, Freddie? Something has to be done! We're not safe here anymore!"

"I'm sure they'll be here soon, mother."

"This is Crystal, and this is April," was Arthur's introduction.

"They're getting bolder all the time!" Flossie was at the windows, frantically worried about the interlopers, hoping to see them again, hoping not to.

"Hello girls," said Astaire.

"Hello Mr. Astaire. You're an honor, I mean we're in honor, I mean—" Crystal was unusually tongue-tied and April was dumbstruck.

"Arthur can't take you back to the city, so we'll call a cab for you..."

"That's very nicely of you," Crystal mumbled incoherently.

Arthur was about to dial for the cab when the front gate phone rang. He answered the intercom. It was the police, and they had the trespassers.

Chapter 46

Pater and dotter reunite

IN A MATTER OF MOMENTS, Arthur buzzed the gate open, and two police cars entered the grounds. Fred Astaire headed straight for the front entrance, and everybody else trouped right out after him. The police wasted no time pulling two men out to face them. They were unsteady on their feet, and appeared dazed.

"Do you know these men, Mr. Astaire?"

"This fellow looks familiar." He stared at Dingle but couldn't quite place him.

Casey was checking them out along with everyone else, but not very intently, since she didn't expect to know them. She didn't recognize her wobbly father. She hadn't seen him for over a decade, since she was a child, so it wasn't surprising.

But Dingle, even in his inebriated state, recognized his daughter immediately.

"Casey! Casey, me girl! Itch yer old dad!"

He dashed up and grabbed her before anyone could stop him. Then everyone grabbed him, startled, trying to pull him away from her.

"Daddy?" Casey said, but it was still a question.

"Shlug tol me yuud be here, darlin'. ITch me, yur deer ol' dad."

"Daddy!" she exclaimed, having given him a more penetrating look. "It is you!"

Astaire, in particular, gave her the most careful look since she'd arrived. She'd hardly said a word or called attention to herself in any way, but now it seemed Casey was the center of everyone's curiosity.

When one of the officer's looked in Harleigh's direction, the amiable black man winked at him. "Sheesh his daughter. We wur waitin'—tomet—to meet— hur."

Their reunion would have proceeded with a little more dignity if they hadn't been skunk drunk, but Arthur was still clear-headed and interrupted the tearful dramatics.

"If these two aren't the trespassers, then they're still lurking around here somewhere..." he addressed the four assembled police-men, momentarily caught up along with everyone else in this unex-pected emotional drama.

They snapped out of it immediately, as if caught sleeping on the job, and started off in a dashing flourish, exchanging a few subtle hand motions with each other, as they began searching the area. But Flossie hadn't been quite as infatuated with the old gent's mush-mouthed greeting as the others. She'd been closely observing the grounds and beyond since leaving the house.

"There they are," she yelled at the top of her voice, pointing toward the road. The trees were sparse on that side of the gate, and two figures were clearly running down the boulevard, away from the house!

Chapter 47

Movie stars in the neighborhood

LENO HAD SPOTTED THEM BEFORE Flossie did, sneaking past the front gate. It had taken Debra and Asher awhile to realize Astaire's property butted the property of other estates, and all of them were securely fenced. The only way in or out of any of them was by the road. He got the cab started and darted out of the driveway just behind them as they started jogging. Asher was still struggling to properly operate his legs in the skirt he wasn't accustomed to wearing.

"Cab, ladies?" Leno leaned out the window to be sure they'd recognize him. If they were surprised to see him, they didn't show it. He stopped and they jumped in the back seat as if the sudden police sirens had triggered rockets in their behinds. He took off with a roar and a cloud of dust, and the race was on.

"Did ja get what you were coming for." Leno asked without taking his eyes off the road ahead. He still had an idea about cutting himself in on whatever it was.

No answer from his nearly hysterical passengers.

There wasn't much traffic in the heights of Bel Air most midafternoons, but the police car close behind was keeping up with him, and Leno was having second thoughts. Though he was an expert driver, he suddenly realized there weren't any turnoffs for miles on this twisting hillside highway, and further flight could only end badly.

"I've gotta stop!" he warned them, with his foot already on the brake.

There was almost no shoulder at all where he came to a full stop. The first police car came up alongside, passed him, and pulled up right in the center of the road. Leno had his arms high in the air as he stepped out of the car, but Asher came out the far side, running, still clutching the towel covered reel under one arm. The two policemen from the second car took off on foot after him as the two from the first car held Leno and Debra at gunpoint. She was still clambering out of the back seat, in slow motion, her disguise all askew.

All of them watched as Asher disappeared off the side of the road, with the two officers following as fast as they could run. Before they even had a chance to put Leno up against the car and frisk him, a bright red Mustang convertible pulled up and the driver called out "Can I help, officers?"

There were a few double takes and a couple of gasps when Leno and the cops recognized Cary Grant at the wheel. The two in uniform were efficient, seasoned policemen, but professionals in every occupation are normally a little starstruck, and freeze for a moment when meeting a major celebrity like this.

Debra would probably have reacted the same way, if she'd also glanced at the conveniently arriving motorist, but as frantic as she was, all she could think of was getting away from the law! In that magic moment when the officers turned their attention to address the legendary movie star, she was in the driver's seat of the cab and tearing off down the road!

It was a desperate act, even if she'd known how to drive, but since she didn't have any experience behind the wheel at all, it was possible, even probable suicide!

She didn't intend to go far, just far enough to escape, then her plan was to jump out and follow Asher's example, to outrun them on foot!

Alas, she mistook the clutch pedal for the brake, and couldn't make the full turn to follow the road, which sent the car blasting through a low picket fence into someone's backyard, onto someone's broad stone patio, and into that same someone's oversize swimming pool, where it sank like a massive boulder.

Debra was unconscious, completely submerged. The woman of the house, standing at her kitchen window, saw it all, and in moments dashed out the back door, ran the few yards to the pool, and dived in. She was an expert swimmer, fortunately, and even more fortunately, the driver door was wide open. It was relatively easy for her to pull Debra out of the car and get her to the surface of the water.

Three men, two of them policemen, one of them with his hand securely holding Jay Leno's shirt cuff, came rushing onto the patio. They were relieved to see the husky housewife straddling Debra, giving artificial respiration, and Debra, who was coughing, cursing, spitting out water, clearly not even close to being badly injured.

The woman got to her feet and made unconscious moves to smooth her attire, but since she was dressed only in a thin, almost transparent white wet robe over a bra and panties, it was a fruitless exercise. Needless to say, she had not been expecting visitors. The scarf over her tangled hair and her slippers had been lost in the water, and she suddenly realized what an indecent indecorous blob she was at the moment.

Leno chose that moment to speak up. "Say, weren't you Esther Williams?"

If looks could kill, Leno would have been charred and gutted guttersnipe.

"No," she snarled, "I'm her mother". But of course, she was Esther Williams. Ten years beyond and at least twenty pounds over her movie star weight, without movie make-up, and with her hair a mottled mess, but in spite of appearing decidedly unbuoyant in her present condition, she was still Esther Williams.

Others were gathering to gape. From the neighborhood. From the road.

"Miss Williams!" Cary Grant exclaimed, "I'm Cary Grant. Can I be of any assistance?"

Esther Williams drew herself to a dignified pose and said "Excuse me," and then she walked with imperious carriage to the back door of her house and exited the scene.

Chapter 48

Distinguished director's hap-
less houseguest

John Huston didn't even particularly like the oddball unemployed movie director he'd met occasionally around his Hollywood haunts, but he had a soft spot for anyone struggling, as he had, to establish himself creatively.

That he was gay didn't factor much into Huston's impression of the man. He was secure enough of his own heterosexual center that he was indifferent to people whose chemical ingredients hadn't been distributed properly at birth.

So, since he was on his way to Africa, on safari, and he knew his casual friend was scratching for rent money for a small apartment in Burbank, he'd generously invited the fellow to stay in his Bel Air house while he was away.

Huston's California abode wasn't a very large or impressive place in comparison to some of his neighbors, like Jimmy Stewart or Fred Astaire, but it had a certain charm. Perched on a measly half acre, the single story residence sat on the side of a steep hill, overlooking Los Angeles. There were many reasons most people wouldn't care for the house at all, but it had a few benefits for a true mystic.

And if ever there was a true mystic, it was Huston's impressionable houseguest.

The view from the sloping backyard, unimpeded by the roofs of homes below the ridge, was a glorious panorama that spread out forever on a clear day. Miles and miles of cityscape, with patches of empty countryside here and there just to give the pattern some diversity. There was enough in view of man's miraculous wonders and nature's grand design to inspire even the most jaded soul.

Huston's house sitter had been standing there for a long time. Dressed casually to an extreme, he was meditating, with half-glazed eyes, his mind racing with the cryptic but insistent orders of the secret society called Ordo Templi Orientalis. He'd purchased a small dog for the sacrifice the day before, and all was in readiness.

The afternoon sun carved out a gradually evolving blanket of shadows over everything from the grass at his feet to the far horizon.

There was a soft breeze, and the world was silent.

Chapter 49

The devil and Kenneth Anger

ASHER SLINKRING, DESPITE THE INHIBITING costume he was wearing, had raced so desperately, so haphazardly, clearing fences and evading all the natural obstacles along the way, that he had eluded his pursuers, at least for the moment. He had been seen though, he knew, by several startled residents in the neighborhood, and probably by a few he didn't know about, so he remained vigilant. Finally, gasping for breath, he turned the corner of a house at a gallop. and came to a dead stop.

Standing a few yards directly in his path was a man in sandals, wearing a robe, head covered by a wide brimmed straw hat. He was standing stock still, in silent meditation, looking out over the valley, which spread for miles in every direction. His back was to the sudden arrival of this unexpected visitor, but he must have heard something, because he turned slowly... and froze in terror at the sight of Asher!

There he was, a monstrous red-eyed giant with electric hair standing in rigid swatches, the big hat and veil long since gone, sweat pouring down his ferocious face, his chest heaving and great effusions of spittle and mucous erupting from his mouth and nostrils. He was still in the dress Debra had so carefully encased him in the day before, but it was ragged now, with rips and tears on every side. His huge feet were bare, and his arms were clutching a bright red towel to his chest. Neither of them said a word for a long minute.

Any normal person would have trouble processing this sudden apparition, but Kenneth Anger was not an ordinary person. Take spiritual to its outer limits and then add another dimension on top of it and you have the complex cortex of the notorious Ken Anger. At some point early in life he'd decided he was a movie director, and the world was so stunned by the originality of his madness that his own self-evaluation was accepted by the Hollywood elite.

'It's the devil' was his immediate conclusion. Who else could it be. This figure had appeared out of thin air, obviously strained and depleted by his arduous journey from the depths of Hell to the alien firmament of earth.

"Welcome," he heard himself utter softly, as if this magnificent creature required human speech from him.

"I need a pair of trousers," Asher declared.

"Of course," Anger said, and extended his hand to guide his magical visitor inside, as if this first utterance of the fallen god made perfect sense.

It was as hot as a sauna inside, which wasn't surprising since there was a fierce, barely confined fire blazing in the fireplace. Asher scarcely noticed the exotic posters on the walls or the many unusual statues strewn about in a pattern meaningful only to his hypnotized host. He needed a pair of pants. Quickly. He knew the police would be there any minute.

"Trousers," he repeated, a little more forcefully this time.

"Of course," Anger repeated, in exactly the same monotone as before, then led Asher into a bedroom, and opened the door of a closet.

The devil looked for the nearest place to deposit his package so he could pull out some hangers and find something to wear. "Is it an offering?" Anger asked meekly, but Asher didn't quite comprehend what he said.

"Very important. Something the world has never seen." he said, but would soon come to regret he hadn't been more specific.

"Is it an offering?" Anger asked again, but Asher didn't answer that question, busy selecting the largest pair of trousers he could find. It wasn't an idle question because coincidentally to the devil's arrival, Anger had finished preparing all the elements for a ritual ceremony and had been outside praying silently, fervently reciting in his own fevered brain the exact phrases of the memorized exultation to the Great Horned One himself before following through with the sacrifice and disposal by fire of the live animal he'd purchased the day before.

Anger returned to the living room, unwrapping the towel from the reel of film. He knew what it was. He read the one word on the tag attached to it. That word was 'Lucifer'.

"Is this a substitute for the dog?" he called out to Asher, who was struggling into a too small pair of trousers, and scarcely processing the man's inane conversation.

"Have you got a car?" Asher ignored the question with one of his own.

"Yes, I have a car, My Lord." Anger was still in thrall, oblivious to the mundane conversation the devil was delivering, so he responded in kind, speaking louder to be sure it carried into the next room. "What is your wish?"

"I need your car," Asher answered, which put a hint of suspicion in the clearing perception of Kenneth Anger. Why would the devil need a car? Couldn't he transport himself wherever he wanted to go, both here on earth or in the blazing interior of the planet?

"Are you Lucifer?" he boldly blurted, bracing for a lighning bolt.

"Lucifer?" Asher had reappeared in the living room, zipping up his fly. He had a shirt over his shoulder and a pair of unlaced shoes on his feet. He looked a great deal less like Lucifer in this common apparel, with a somewhat less horrific expression on his face, and other evidence of human origin. "Do I look that bad?"

"Who are you?" Anger demanded. He was back in reality with a lurch, as suddenly as he'd been transported into fantasyland.

"Doesn't matter," Asher mumbled, "I'm in a jam. I need your car."

"I don't think so," Anger replied, "Get out!"

"Give me my film," Asher held out his hand.

Anger retreated a few steps, clutching the reel closer than ever.

Asher rushed. The reel spun in the air and dropped neatly into the center of the fireplace, exploding immediately into a burst of blue flame and smoke that denied any chance of retrieving it.

'Oh NO!" Asher gasped. He watched the popping acetate melt and disappear in a matter of moments.

Anger was oblivious to the loss, his emotions churning, both angry and disappointed at this sudden turn of events. It was just an ugly mortal misadventure, not the grand spiritual illumination he'd perceived it to be only a few minutes earlier.

"You fool," Asher threatened the rapidly recuperating director. "I oughta break your neck! Debra will be furious. She'll cut me loose now. I'm doomed." But his fury evaporated as soon as it came to the surface, and he fell back disconsolately on the couch, almost in tears.

As if on cue, the front doorbell rang. Asher was alert enough to realize his situation. He knew the police were there within a few steps, ready to take him into custody.

Anger was alert enough too. "The bedroom." he jerked his thumb in that direction.

It was the police. They wanted to know if Mr. Anger had seen anybody running through the neighborhood. Mr. Anger told them he hadn't, and they left.

Asher was in the closet with the door closed.

"Come out, you phony devil," Anger spoke to the door, "The police have gone."

Chapter 50

The whole gang hops to the hoofer's house

Arthur left a note for the police on the gate, with Gene Kelly's phone number, as the entire party set out for the anticipated premiere of Jessie Matthew's secret production. They had to take two cars because there were so many in the group now. Dingle and Harleigh had to be included, of course, especially after Astaire recognized Thimble as a casual pal from the track, a respected tout, in Astaire's mind, who knew what mood a horse was in just by looking at it. The Goldcurls twins had to be invited, simply because nobody could figure out what to do with them, and besides, they'd pleaded, with the most gooey flattery to convince their host they'd be so honored to see anything at all in which he had a part. Flossie drove the Lincoln. She absolutely refused to remain alone in the house, with only the cook and the maid, in case those awful trespassers returned. Her son was a licensed driver, but few who'd been a passenger when he was behind the wheel would dare chance that experience again. He was always off in a dream, scarcely aware of other vehicles around him, and prone to getting lost even on usual routes in and out of the city.

They turned the curve around the Fernando Lamas property carefully, observing the broken fence and police cars on the road near his driveway. All of them assumed it was the apprehension of their trespassers, but decided not to stop. There was nothing they could do, and they were confident the police would advise them in due course about what should be done about preferring charges.

"Isn't that Cary Grant's convertible," Astaire wondered aloud, "I wonder what he's doing there." Grant had been one of the guests at a recent dinner party at Doris Day's house, and he'd insisted on giving several of them a ride in his new car, the old hoofer included. It was an added hazard at the turn, barely off onto the shoulder of the road at all.

Doris Day, what a peach. Now there's a girl he would have liked to dance with. They would have been such a natural combination on screen. She might not have been quite as good a dancer as Ginger, but certainly a far superior singer. He watched her half hour TV show faithfully every week, and marveled at her bouncy personality, even then, in her 50's. What a different film 'Let's Dance' would have been, with Doris instead of Betty Hutton as his costar. Ah well... He was lost in a wonderful 'What if?' all the way to Kelly's house.

"Here we are, sir," Arthur announced. He could see his boss was shaking himself out of a faraway dreamland.

Kelly was leaping gracefully off the front steps before they were all out of the cars. He was momentarily startled to see so many, but took it in stride, rushing up to Astaire and giving him a big hug. "Fred, old buddy!" He exclaimed. They lived within a couple of miles but hadn't actually been face to face in...well... years.

The introductions, once they were inside, took quite awhile, and were a bit awkward, due to the fact that the still fresh acquaintances came from such diverse areas of the universe. Casey was totally caught up in intimate reminiscing with her dear old long lost daddy, and Robert, just as he had been at the first showing of the film, felt completely out of place, as totally alone as he ever had been in his life.

Cyd Charisse was there with her husband, Tony Martin, two of the foursome for golf this substituted gathering had aborted. "Cyd!" Astaire exclaimed when he saw her, "You doll! As beautiful as ever. Even More. My dream girl!" Well, he'd spent considerable time in cloudland with Cyd too.

"Hello Fred," Tony Martin extended his hand. He just wanted to remind the old man he was in attendance too.

"I'm hardly a dream like this, without any make-up or anything." Cyd protested, a bit embarrassed by his effusive greeting. Her hair was tied up in a bun, under a cap to keep it in place, and she had on a shapeless sweater and a loose fitting pair of slacks, the appropriate attire for golf with a bunch of guys. "I'm ugly today."

"Ugly! He was still fast on the uptake. "The best make-up team at MGM couldn't make you look ugly no matter how hard they tried."

She laughed out loud at that line, and other introductions followed.

Donald O'Conner, the fourth of the foursome that day, was in ebullient spirits, as usual. He went into an impromtu dance, and finished by grabbing Kelly and Astaire in a bear hug. "The three of us, together at last. What do you say we do a musical together. Cyd can be one of the girls, along with..." he paused, trying to come up with any feminine stars still on their feet.

"How about Doris Day?" Astaire volunteered.

"Perfect," O'Conner laughed.

"And Carol Burnett," Kelly put an immediate frown on O'Conner's puss.

"I suppose she'd be my partner," he sighed. Although the whole scenario had come to him in a flash, it wasn't far from similar plot plans that had been occurring to also ran' O'Conner since the high point of his career, doing 'Make 'em Laugh', his knockout single in Singing in the Rain with Kelly two decades earlier.

At some point, Astaire introduced Robert to the group, and a hush settled over the crowd as if a giant wet blanket had descended from the ceiling.

As Astaire had remembered, Kelly directed everyone into the projection room, a room with seats exactly like those in any neighborhood movie theater, a room designed expressly for the showing of movies. Kelly did have one in-house all-around assistant, who had been pressed into extra duty, popping several bags of popcorn and soon serving iced soft drinks all around. A young aspiring dancer, naturally, named Ernie Elfludger (It would have to be changed if he ever hoped to make it in show business) was also their projectionist.

Finally everyone was seated, and quieted down along with the lights. Robert noticed the dim pink side lights along the wall and marveled at Kelly's attention to detail in designing this intimate home theater.

Thimble and O'Halloran, still tipsy but sobering up after the ride, were the last to stop laughing and carrying on, both of them thoroughly enjoying the occasion.

What Robert had hoped would be a strictly private showing for Astaire alone had evolved into a mob scene, most of them totaling unsuspecting of what they were about to see. If the majority opinion was negative, derisive of the antique aspects of the barely professional settings and overall production, it might easily affect Astaire's perception. He suddenly realized he was deep in depression, and had been gradually approaching this sad state of mind ever since meeting the great man that morning. Nothing had gone right up to this point, and all manner of further disasters were forming in his imagination. He stole a glance at Casey, who looked like she was every bit as content as a pregnant cow in a quiet sunlit meadow. The others all appeared to be cheerfully expectant too.

The projector came to life with a roar, and the credits began to roll. For a catch-as-catch-can, off-the-cuff movie, Jessie had obviously been a popular gal in those days. Apparently every department in the small British studio had pitched in to provide their unique individual talents, adding expert complements to the barely credible screenplay. The credits, for example, were a delightful blend of inventive art deco typography and cute cartoons. No stinting there. As clever as any top musical of the day.

The plot, as basic as it was, had Astaire, (the hero, a musical star from America, on holiday in London, playing a character named Fred Astaire) meeting a maid (Jessie Matthews, an aspiring dancer named Jessie Matthews) in his hotel. She does everything she can to impress him, singing and dancing in various situations, but he thinks she's batty. Gradually he realizes she really does have talent, and they end up dancing together right up to the closing curtain on a grand London stage, accompanied by loud and vigorous applause. They'd used every foot of film they'd shot of Astaire, and set up unobtrusive back shots of his character using a slim actor who looked exactly like him from behind. Then they'd thrown in a few comedy bits, which were easy to do, there being at least as many low comedy hams in England in those days as in Hollywood. The rest was all Jessie Matthews, and she was at her very best, maybe even better than her best because there wasn't any director or producer second guessing her every move. She was free to improvise every dance step, and sing the songs she liked until she alone was satisfied.

As the film began, Robert began to pull out of his droop. It was so much smoother without the tics and ragged editing so noticeable at the first showing. It was still pretty old, rather gray, without the sharp blacks and whites it needed. That too, could be rectified, he knew. And surely Astaire would realize it as well.

The audience had quieted, as absorbed, Robert hoped, as he'd been upon seeing it for the first time. The biggest laugh and most audience wisecracks came during the scene in which Jessie, innocently sexy, sat covered in foaming soapsuds during a bubble bath, singing a delightfully inappropriate song titled 'Look At Me Now'.

The movie lasted only a few minutes over an hour, and when it ended there came a generous burst of clapping and cheers from all assembled. All except Fred Astaire. Kelly was the first to plant himself in front of the old master, find a hand sitting limply in his lap and shake it vigorously.

"It's a classic, Fred. A little gem! It needs a few touches, but it's charming as it is! I've gotta call Stan Donen.! He's gotta see this! He can put in some special effects that will really jazz it up!"

"Pornography!" Astaire blurted so forcefully that it stopped all the chatter in the background, interrupting everyone's exchanges about what they'd just seen. It was such an unexpected word, and so demonstrably delivered that few believed they'd heard the word they'd heard.

"Pornography?" Donald O'Conner said. He was sitting to Astaire's left.

"Pornography?" Tony Martin repeated. He was sitting next to his wife, who was sitting right next to her dear old costar.

"In the bathtub!" Astaire was on his feet now. "I saw her nipples! Twice! Pornography! I won't allow this picture to be shown!"

For a few moments, no one knew what to say. Robert certainly didn't, and wouldn't, even if he did.

Somebody started to laugh, but cut if off quickly, realizing Astaire was deadly serious.

"Fred, that's not pornography. Not even close." Kelly tried reason, but it was too soon.

"You saw it, didn't you, Cyd?" Her hero looked directly at her, seeking affirmation of his intemperate charge.

She cringed, on the spot, not wanting to contradict him, but couldn't betray her own immediate reaction, "I... don't think it was pornographic, Fred. I don't think so."

Cyd Charisse had long enjoyed a reputation as a very proper lady, but she was in truth quite liberal and hardly offended by the brief sight of a nipple. Suddenly she had a flash memory of the nearly naked scene she'd done for the film 'The Silencers' a couple of years earlier. Had Fred seen that, she wondered. In the movie, behind the credits, she'd performed a strip that showed more skin than she'd ever shown the public before, hot enough to earn an 'R' rating from the censors. She valued the respect Astaire held for her, so now she was experiencing a flush of shame, hoping it hadn't been compromised.

"Fred, you're overreacting." Tony Martin thought he'd try to bring a little perspective to the subject. "People are running around naked in lots of movies these days. Times have changed."

"I have a certain reputation," Astaire had at least recovered a normal tone of voice. "When people see one of my pictures, they know it's 'G' rated."

So, he did know about the rating system. That was a start.

"That scene could be edited. The nipples can be erased." Kelly asserted firmly.

That's right, Fred," Cyd said, her hand on his arm as he sat back down.

"I didn't like some of that dialogue in the comedy scenes either," he went on, "Very vulgar. And some of those lyrics were too suggestive. Noel Coward was a sexual deviate, and he liked to put… dirty innuendos… in his lyrics."

"Is he still alive?" O'Conner wondered, as if it had any bearing on the discussion.

"I think so," Tony Martin, the old crooner, would have remembered if he'd seen an obituary notice for a composer of Coward's stature.

Robert blanched another shade of gray. He hadn't even thought about Coward. Would he have to get his authorization too?

Normally Astaire was careful to keep his conservative opinions to himself. He knew most of Hollywood had always been populated mostly with flaming liberals... and libertines! But here he was, brought up suddenly by a ghost from his barely remembered history that was in danger of coming back to life and roaming about in the comfortable past and present of his settled reality.

It was probably for the best that a phone began ringing as others were preparing to join the main conversation, since their own, up to this point, were merely mumbled asides to each other.

"It's the police, Mr. Kelly" Ernie announced over the din. "It's for Mr. Astaire."

Chapter 51

Esther and Cary costar off camera

ESTHER WILLIAMS REGAINED HER COMPOSURE as soon as she was back inside her house, but her next thought came with a shudder, a dread of the predictable reaction of her husband, Fernando Lamas, when he got home to find a car in his swimming pool, not to mention the other incidental damage to his property. His anger would be explosive, and it would surely be directed at her, she knew, as irrational as that would be. Lamas had many fine qualities, but he was less tolerant of any disturbances to himself or his belongings than the ordinary fellow, which Esther had discovered in their few years together. She didn't want to be home when he arrived, which would be only a few hours later.

She looked out the kitchen window. Cary Grant was still loitering around, looking very tentative.

She unhooked the latch and pushed the window open. He must have good hearing, she thought, because, at least thirty feet away, he turned to look directly at her.

"Do you still want to help me?" she called out.

"Of course. Anything." he called back.

"Give me fifteen minutes," she made sure he heard that, and rushed to her bedroom. Normally she could spif up in ten minutes, but in this case she had to start at the top and work all the way down. It took her every one of those fifteen minutes, but when she reappeared through the back door onto the patio, she was definitely, no mistake, Esther Williams the movie star. It was an uncanny transformation. Cary Grant began beaming when he saw her, and she beamed right back.

The police were still there, stringing tape and taking photos, and Debra was on her feet, in handcuffs, sniffling and cursing, even more disheveled than Esther had been, her dress loose and torn, all of the padding having fallen out, floated out or simply disintegrated.

"You won't need me for anything, will you?" Esther asked the nearest cop.

"We need your name and phone number, in case you're wanted as a witness, and I'll give you a number you can call about insurance claims. You know, our report for your insurance company."

That was taken care of, and within minutes Cary and Esther were speeding away in his beautiful red convertible toward Malibu where he knew about a comfortable private resort which had an exclusive dining room with secluded bowered booths where they could relax without having to endure the mawkish adulation of the unwashed public. The public wasn't really that much of a nuisance since their long absence from the screen, but by habit they pretended to themselves they were still potent celebrities.

"I had a crush on you. I wanted to make a movie with you.." Cary declared, in all seriousness.

Esther just laughed.

"It's true. When I saw that one where Peter Lawford kidnapped you and flew you to that island..."

"'On An Island With You'," Esther supplied the title. "That was one of my favorites. It had everything. Lovely music by Xaviar Cugat... that dear funny Jimmy Durante..."

"I could have done that part as good as Peter Lawford," Cary asserted without a trace of humor or any sense of how foolish it sounded.

"Of course you could. I would have loved to have made a movie with you," she responded, just as if their dialogue wasn't a little bit silly, verging on ridiculous.

"My wife wouldn't let me. Well, she didn't exactly have veto power about what roles I took, but she could be pretty persuasive."

"Which wife was that?"

"Betsy Palmer. I outweighed her by a good 50 pounds, but she was the heavyweight in our relationship. She knew exactly every move she should make and every move I should make. I didn't mind much. She was usually right. But she became too everbearing as time went on. Nice girl, Betsy. I talk to her occasionally."

Esther was quickly realizing that Cary Grant was a babbler, an elegant, distinguished old windbag!

"She told me I couldn't be in one of your movies because you were the solitary star of any Esther Williams swimming movie," Cary went on, "and your leading men were inevitably just supporting players. I had to admit she was right."

"I don't think you were ever anything but the leading man, were you?"

"I was definitely a supporting player in that early Mae West movie," Cary had a marvelous memory among his many other attributes, "Miss West couldn't have been upstaged by a whole circus in those days."

"Too bad." Esther mused in agreement, "I would have loved making a movie with you. It would have been okay with me if your name was above the title and I had tenth billing below a trained dolphin."

Cary Grant was a good laugher, and that ad lib was a corker. She laughed too, all the mess at her house forgotten as they coplotted a fantasy screenplay.

"I can swim well enough, you know," he bragged, "That wouldn't have been a problem. I could swim better than Peter Lawford with one arm and one leg tied behind my back."

After awhile, they were reduced to giggles.

They'd reached the resort. As the subtly celestial couple made their way to the restaurant, few passersby even recognized them. The hostess did recognize Grant, a regular, and made just enough of a fuss to show that she did, but not enough to alert the other diners. There weren't many people in the place then early afternoon, after lunch, before the dinner hour.

"Where were you headed today when you took the detour to my place." Esther asked him, ignoring any mention of the dramatic accident that brought them together.

He hesitated, which in itself was revealing. Babbler Grant was seldom at a loss for words. "I was on my way to see my… doctor," he finally confessed. At least it seemed to be a confession.

"Oh," Esther paused, preparing to change the subject immediately.

"Oh, not a regular doctor," he hastily explained, "A head doctor. Well, not a head doctor either."

"A witch doctor maybe?" Esther was joking, but actually not far from the truth.

"Close enough, I guess," Cary laughed. I've been taking an experimental drug, under a doctor's supervision, for awhile now."

"What's it supposed to do for you?" was her next natural question.

They ordered drinks, exotic intoxicating alcoholic drinks, and took notice of the soft but lush melodic music in the background that added an extra dimension to the atmosphere. It was just recorded music, wafting through carefully placed speakers, but effective. Cary Grant did indeed know where to take a lady on a romantic rendezvous.

Oddly, his conversation, unscripted by talented screenwriters, didn't match the matchless prose he had delivered so convincingly on the screen for decades, aging beautifully along the way, more attractive to the opposite sex when he retired than he'd ever been before. In fact, he was coming off as a rather curious combination of deficiencies.

Esther, a down-to-earth woman without any neuroses at all, was intrigued but not in the least infatuated. She was no spring chicken herself, but he did seem like a goofy grandfather to her. She braced herself for further revelations, and was ready for a second drink before he was.

"I was raped when I was 14 years old," he came up with that revelation right out of the blue. She waited for the rest of it.

"I was part of a troupe of acrobats, We toured all over England, Scotland, on vaudeville stages, in circuses. A girl, a young chorus girl, she was three years older, took a fancy to me, I guess. She got me alone and raped me."

"She raped you? How could that happen? I mean, you must have been agreeable..."

"I didn't know anything about sex. It terrified me. I didn't have any idea a girl could be that... hot for sex."

"But if you were terrified, how could you... you know... get it up?"

He paused for moment, deciding on the word he'd use to explain. "Let's just say, she violated me. I wasn't into it at all."

I cried when it was over. Then she cried too, when she saw me crying.

"It made a lasting impression, I guess," Esther volunteered.

"She wasn't a bad sort, really. She bought me a big bag of Cadbury Crunchies the next day."

"Cadbury Crunchies?" Esther grinned, "Was that a special treat?"

"Those Crunchies were the most delicious candies in the whole world. There's nothing comparable in the states. So I forgave her, I guess." Now it was his turn to grin.

"Did you ever see her again?"

"No, but I should have. She became a big star in English movies a few years later. Her name was Jessie Matthews. Ever hear of her?"

"I don't think so," Esther wondered what this story had to do with anything.

"It confused me. That incident with her. Ever since that early episode I've been a little intimidated by women, confused. All my life."

"I was raped too, at about the same age." she hadn't meant to bring that up. but it was out of her mouth before she could pull it back into her fading memory.

"Really?" he was fully prepared to hear the details. But she wasn't eager to give them up, and cut the story short.

"It didn't confuse me at all." she insisted, "It just made me realize what men wanted, and made me determined to be the one who decided when they got it."

"I guess everybody has a more complicated life than..."

"More complicated than they want others to know about," she finished his thought, hoping he'd take the hint.

"Have you ever heard of LSD?" he sort of whispered the word, hinting he knew it was not only potentially dangerous, but illegal.

"I've heard of it," was all she could think to say. Was Cary Grant a dope fiend?

"I think it's done me some good. Not sure, but I think so."

"What's it supposed to do for you?" He still hadn't answered that question.

"I'm trying to find out who I am." But he apparently wasn't yet ready to answer her question. "I've been trying for quite a long time."

What was this all about? He had volunteered to help **her** this afternoon, but the conversation was getting very heavy, and it was all about **him**! Esther felt like she was being placed in the unlikely role of counselor, a role in which she'd had no previous experience.

"I'm a goofy kind of a guy," he continued, oblivious of her slightly retreating attitude, "I like to do silly things, and make people laugh. I like to help people, like doing housework, or helping a neighbor build a doghouse, or paint a fence. But people won't let me do those things. They stop me right away and say 'You shouldn't do those things. You're a big movie star. Go sit on your throne and let us take care of these trivial chores.'"

"Oh, come on, Cary," she couldn't help herself. It was just too absurd.

"I'm only Cary Grant when I'm working." he blurted. Now a few of the not many other diners were looking in their direction. "Most of the time I'm Archie Leach! I walked on stilts for years, not because I had to but because I liked it!"

Esther was speechless, and suddenly he realized he'd gone too far. Cary Grant regained control, and when next he spoke it was in the smooth confident tone the world would recognize.

"I'm sorry," he said, "it's because the subject of LSD came up, and I know that's controversial. You're very empathic, or at least you seem to be, and I'm taking advantage."

"Well, Archie, old fellow," she was loosening up after two sturdy drinks, and felt compelled to comment, "I think I understand your predicament." She almost pronounced the word properly, not drunk enough yet to slur her words.

"You're rich, talented, admired by millions of men, adored by millions of women, but inside, you don't think you measure up. Well, here's my advice:" She leaned forward, right in his face, and made it a husky whisper she knew he'd remember, "Learn to live with it!"

He'd remember alright. For the moment, he was just embarrassed. During the ride back to Bel Air, they talked about Esther's life, all about her early life, how she got into show business, her marriages, mostly about her current marriage with Lamas, who had a formidable reputation himself.

"You know, Cary, we do have a lot in common. Because of my looks, other people were pushing me into a career before I'd decided for myself what I wanted to do, how I wanted to live." Despite the harrowing events of earlier in the day, she was feeling mellow and philosophic, watching a colorful sunset as they drove along.

"Not me. I was in my thirties before things started happening for me. It was a long, slow slog."

"Well, even so, I'll bet you were surprised yourself, the first time you saw yourself on screen and realized how you came across."

"Not the first time," he knew exactly what she meant, "but the first serious part..."

"I never thought much about my looks," she was on a roll now, "I was just so fixated on my swimming. I wanted to go to the Olympics and swim faster than anybody else on the planet."

Cary ignored her, and went on with the recollection she'd dug out of his crowded memory. "I was a cipher in my first few pictures, but when I made a movie called 'Blonde Venus' with Marlene Dietrich, in 1932, I was really forceful and confident. I couldn't believe it was me."

Esther was leading up to making a point of her own. "I was surprised when I first saw myself on film," she continued, "I only had a small part in an Andy Hardy movie, but up until then I didn't know I was that pretty."

"C'mon, you're kidding." Grant did hear that remark, but didn't believe it. "Girls start looking in mirrors as soon as they're out of diapers."

"Well, not quite that early," she chuckled, "but you're not far wrong. I knew I was okay—"

"Okay?" he challenged.

"Okay, maybe I knew I was a little above average, but I didn't think I had movie star looks."

"I don't think most people know what they look like to others."

"I'm sure you're right," she agreed. Then she got to the point of her monologue. "For most of my life, I was trying to satisfy the public, the anonymous public, but I finally realized the public wasn't giving anything back."

"Is that really how you feel? I still get stopped for autographs... I get letters."

"Oh, they paid hard cash to see my movies, and that brought me material things, but not one dime's worth of affection or love. I asked myself what I wanted, and the answer was pretty basic. I didn't want mobs of people to love me from afar, I just wanted one man who loved the real me, an ordinary woman."

"You're right, of course," Cary said softly, "That's it in a nutshell. I've been married five times, you know." He figured that alone was proof enough he knew what she was talking about.

"I found my man, a strong, self-confident man," She'd just about reached the end of her long-winded exposition, "and my career now is just a pleasant memory."

Motor mouth Grant let that pass without a response. He knew she'd have a capper to finish her unexpected monologue.

"I treat him like a king, and he treats me like a queen. I serve him like a slave, and he serves me—"

"I hope there aren't any chains involved." Cary interrupted, clearly wondering.

"No chains, Cary. It's all in the mind. I married another actor, and maybe we're both playing dual roles fulltime, but it works for us."

"Are you trying to tell me something?"

"I was just trying to say how alike we are. Being a movie star is rewarding in many ways, but it's not the answer to everything. You've really got to stop worrying about what the public thinks of you."

"You know something..." he turned from traffic to look straight into her eyes with the conviction that had transfixed generations of adoring females, "You're right."

She knew Lamas would have been home for an hour or two by the time she got back, enough time for his initial rage to subside. She knew how to settle him down from that point on, and was eager for the challenge.

Cary Grant stopped taking LSD soon after their one and only date, and Esther Williams tried it... just once. Having survived the cataclysmic final water skiing, high diving, fountain spouting. Technicolor water extravaganza to bring 'Easy to Love' to a gigantic climax, no hallucinogenic drug could compare with an experience like that.

Chapter 52

The end of a hectic day

WHEN THE WHOLE MOB GOT back safely to Astaire's gate, a few partings were in order. Arthur took the Goldcurl girls back to the city in the limousine. Their adventure had ended successfully when Gene Kelly took their phone number and promised to keep them in mind.... what more could they ask for? To hell with Murgin's slimy plan for them to steal the film. He wouldn't have been able to do anything with it even if they had.

Casey's farewell to her dad was a little more emotional, but she handled it well, and promises were made to get together again before she left California. Harleigh's old Chevy was still parked on the shoulder of the road, as it had been since that morning. No thief had been tempted to hotwire it and drive it away, and the police in the area had been too busy with other matters to bother issuing a traffic ticket.

Astaire agreed to meet with Robert and Casey again the next day, giving him time to make a decision, one way or the other. He'd promised the whole crowd to think it over until then, at least.

Two policemen in one car had been patiently waiting with two miscreants, and remained patient while Astaire unlocked the gate, enabling his mother to drive the Lincoln back into the garage. Finally, as the rest of them were deciding how to conclude their business, the officers approached the head of the household in an official manner and one of them said "Mr. Astaire, we caught one of the two trespassers, who says she's associated with one of your guests."

"One of... these people?" He looked around, trying to discern the object of their insinuation.

"A Robert Traburt."

"Who, me?" This was completely astounding.

"Are you Robert Traburt?"

"Trabur," Robert corrected him.

"Do you know this woman?"

The other officer was approaching with a drastically disheveled Debra. Robert had never seen her this way, and could barely recognize her at all. Add the fact that she was the last person he expected to see here and it's understandable he was tongue-tied until after she confirmed her identity."

"Robert, there's been a terrible mistake!"

"Debra... What are you doing here?"

"Robert, you brought me along to help you on this trip. Tell them I'm here with you."

He paused but knew all eyes were on him, and he had to say something. Here was the love of his life, involved in some mischief he knew nothing about, pleading for his absolution.

"I know this woman," he said. "What's she done?"

"So far as we know, she trespassed here, with another person. Is that all, Mr. Astaire? Did she steal anything?" the senior officer inquired.

"I don't think so," he replied. No one had seen Asher enter the house and abscond with the film.

"Well, she escaped from police custody," the officer continued, "and crashed this man's cab through a fence into a swimming pool." He hooked his thumb at Jay Leno, who was ambling up, unescorted by any officer, having successfully convinced them he had simply picked up two pedestrians and was completely innocent of any complicity in their affairs. They were through with him, officially, but had offered him a ride back to the city when they were through with Astaire.

"She isn't carrying any identification. Was she here with you or—"

"I'll be responsible for her," if that's what this is leading up to." Robert interrupted the officer. His amazement was fading, and he was beginning to suspect the basic circumstances of her appearance, however inexplicably devious and destructive.

"Mr. Trabur," Astaire groaned, "I'm going to let you sort this out. I'm going in now. I need to sit down. Or lie down. Let me know how it all works out."

He started for the house, and James Ames, still in attendance, followed close behind. Flossie met her son at the door, and her expression was unusually hostile, directed at Debra of course.

Casey kept her mouth shut throughout. Her own disruptive family business had come and gone without undue injury or anguish, so she felt relieved that this much more devastating development far overwhelmed her own. She was curious, though, and paid close attention to everything then transpiring between the law, the girlfriend and her partner Robert.

After Robert had supplied Debra's full name, address, phone number and a few additional details, as well as his own, the police, obviously relieved to have brought the whole thing to a reasonable conclusion, were glad to leave her in Robert's care, and be able to go on their way, their day, plus overtime, over and out. She'd be getting a summons to appear in court, so she couldn't leave the state. Mr. Astaire had to know exactly where she could be located, since he was the only party with an established local address.

"Be seein' ya, sister auntie," Leno flipped her a crook of his middle finger as he left.

Chapter 53

An agent makes himself useful

IT WAS WELL AFTER DARK by the time James Ames pulled out of the Astaire grounds and headed back to the city. Robert sat beside him, Casey and Debra were in the back seat exchanging sullen glances. Ames had generously offered to take them to a hotel for the night, or probably several nights before they could return east.

"I've persuaded Mr. Astaire to give it serious thought before he rejects your proposal entirely, Mr. Trabur," Ames assured Robert, "I think It would be the best thing for his career if he followed through with it, and agreed to the release of the film."

An unexpected ally! Robert winked at Casey over his shoulder, and she smiled. It didn't matter to her one way or another if the old picture show was ever seen again, but Robert had put so much effort into the project that she hoped for his sake it would turn out the way he wanted it to. Her feelings for him were a surprise to her, and she wasn't sure when her initial aversion had turned to a grudging respect.

"He's lost his star power, and doesn't seem to care," Ames continued, as if everyone else cared as much as he did. "He's been doing these little TV shows lately, but if this Jessie Matthews movie hit the screens, it would be a sensation. He'd be back getting A picture scripts!"

He hadn't said much earlier in the day, when everybody else had an opinion, but James Ames was a rare kind of an agent. Robert had no way of knowing, but he didn't say much, even when pitching a client to a prospective employer. Producers were often perplexed at how little bombast he delivered in conversation, often leaving the impression his clients were busy and unconcerned but just might accept a role if all the conditions were right. Of course, he had a small client list, and they were all top people who didn't need a big build-up.

They'd reached a busy multi-laned boulevard, and the lights of the city were suddenly surrounding them.

"How serious do you think the case is going to be against Miss Lavish?" It was uppermost in Robert's mind at the moment, and Ames was a player in this city. He might know what their next move should be.

"I'll call Esther Williams tomorrow morning, and try to smooth things out for you. I know her, she's a reasonable gal. You should probably go see her, check out the damage there. If you want to guarantee all costs to repair the pool, the fence... she should agree not to press charges."

"And the cab company. I should go there and agree to pay to get the cab repaired."

"I'm not too busy tomorrow. I'll drive you."

What a sport, that James Ames! And he'd been so stern at the outset.

"Are you listening, Debra?" Robert spoke louder, without bothering to turn around to look at her. "You're going to be responsible for these costs eventually, you know."

"I hear you," she grumbled.

"If nobody makes a complaint, the only thing they have against the girl is attempted escape. And since she hadn't yet been advised that she was under arrest... That's right, isn't it, Miss Lavish?"

"That's right," another almost inaudible response.

"It's a relatively minor misdemeanor. There'll be a fine, of course, and that could be a few hundred dollars," Over the years, Ames had represented a number of willful juvenile and irresponsible adult actors who'd committed far worse offenses.

Arthur hadn't yet discovered the missing film Asher had stolen, but even if or when that happened, it was such an unimportant object that Astaire probably wouldn't bother to report it to the police.

Ames delivered them to what he knew to be an acceptable hotel near his office, and promised to call the next morning.

"We're all invited to Astaire's for dinner tomorrow night, including Miss Lavish." he waved cheerily, "He'll give you his decision about the film then."

They all realized Miss Lavish couldn't be trusted to be left alone.

The desk clerk was warily suspicious of this shaggy trio without luggage, particularly Debra, still the unkempt disaster she'd been after being dragged up out of Esther Williams' pool. Her torn and dirty dress was about three sizes too big now that the padding had been lost along the way. But Robert gave a brief convincing explanation of why they were in this condition, and they eventually acquired two adjoining rooms, one for him, one for the girls. Nothing was said, but Casey naturally assumed she would be guarding Debra, just in case the dingbat decided to slip out and disappear before dawn. She chose the bed nearest the door and took the added precaution of placing a heavy chair against it.

Chapter 54

Kelly and Astaire, Astaire and Kelly

"Fred, you're not a prude! What's the real reason you're so upset about this old movie?" Gene Kelly had arrived early the next morning by himself, and demanded a private audience with his dear friend of three eventful decades. Astaire had the look of a man with a severe case of gastritis complicated by twisted nuts and a tied tongue. But Gene was relentless, and finally the old hoofer confessed his real anxiety.

"What I did in that film was just a cliché reprise of old steps I'd done on the stage for years, nothing original or clever at all. We didn't rehearse anything! It was just a home movie!"

"But the audience will know that. They won't compare it to your classics. But it's still charming. And Jessie Matthews is delightful!"

"All true," Astaire sighed, "and that's just it. She steals the whole show. She didn't rehearse the numbers in her own movies! She told me! The director would say, 'Dance, Jessie', and she'd just spin and kick and make it up as she went along. She had natural grace, and the public loved her. How could I compete with that?"

Kelly erupted in a loud guffaw. "Fred, old man, you're worrying about nothing. "Natural grace"? That's why men are attracted to an ordinary woman walking down the street. They're the graceful sex!"

"Ginger rehearsed as much as I did." he growled, nowhere near mollified. "And Jessie, even if she didn't, could do as many takes as she wanted to for this pick-up production before she was satisfied."

But Kelly just wouldn't give up. "Granted, she's the main attraction. She had months to work on this thing after you'd left town. Everyone will understand what a minor part you had in it... but they'll love seeing the rare bits, never seen before, from your prime!"

"You know how hard I worked on those dances, those long hours of practice and rehearsal, until we had it perfect." Astaire sulked, "and then take after take. And I had Hermes Pan there with me, on every number, not only to help me create the steps, but to make sure I didn't make any fay moves."

"Well, you've got a point there, Fred, I'll admit. I had to be careful of that too."

"Girls have it easy. They don't have to worry about looking queer while dancing."

"So long as they don't look awkward." Kelly was trying to humor his pal, without much success.

You're as much or more of a perfectionist than I am, Gene! I've heard about how hard you are on your dancing partners!"

"I know. I give up. What more can I say."

"You give up?" he looked up with a hint of a smile, "Well, good. Since you're here, how about joining me for breakfast?" His visitor had arrived so early, this early riser hadn't even had time to do his morning exercises, a routine he tried never to miss. Today, he'd skip it.

"Speaking about rehearsals, I have to be at NBC at ten. I'm gonna be on the Dean Martin show next Saturday." He looked at his watch. "That's why I came so early. I wanted to talk to you before you made a hasty decision."

"You've got time for breakfast." He pulled a cord near the window, and Arthur responded within a couple of minutes. Well, with a celebrity visitor in the study, he was loitering just outside the door, prepared for Astaire's summons. He actually paused for a full 60 seconds, just to provide the impression he had been elsewhere in the house attending to important butler duties.

They gave Arthur their breakfast selections, and he hastened on his way to the cook, while Astaire and Kelly ambled to the dining room.

"Times have changed, Fred," apparently he hadn't given up, after all. "People don't put in all that preparation any more. Spontaneity is the thing these days. Dean Martin doesn't rehearse at all! I'll be there today with the rest of the week's guests, and the regulars, going over songs with the band, blocking the scenes, but Martin won't even be there!"

"Yeah, I've heard he was lazy."

"He comes in on tape day, they give him a general idea of who's there and what he's supposed to do, and he just wings it! If he forgets his lyrics or falls off the piano, the audience just laughs, like it's part of the act. It IS part of his act!"

"I've seen his show. He gets away with it. But dancing is different."

Now Kelly really was through.

"You're going to squelch this film, aren't you," he sighed, resignedly as Arthur appeared to deliver juice and pour coffee,

"I haven't decided yet," Astaire said, and then changed the subject.

Chapter 55

Ditzy doll makes a getaway!

THE HOTEL WAS IN THE center of Los Angeles, within walking distance of any kind of shop or business they needed, so Casey hustled Debra to the closest clothing store even before thinking of breakfast. She looked a bit better after combing her hair, but that oversize dress was still an eyesore. Casey found another outfit for herself as Debra tried on a couple of dresses in the fitting room, and, thanks to the loans Robert had provided for each of them, paid for her purchase in cash. She waited for several minutes without any concern, but suddenly she realized the girl wasn't anywhere in sight. Quickly checking the fitting rooms, Casey confirmed she wasn't in the store at all!

"The girl who came in with me," Casey almost knocked over a salesgirl, "Where did she go?"

"She handed me a twenty dollar bill, and rushed out. She didn't even wait for a receipt or her change."

"Did you see which way she went?" That was definitely a longshot.

"No I didn't. Do you want the dress she came in wearing?"

Casey was already racing for the front door, and didn't bother to respond. Once outside on the sidewalk, she looked in both directions, knowing there'd been ample time for Debra to disappear. Her heart sank. Robert would be liable for all of Debra's disasters, and probably lose his job! No time to think about that... she had to find that witch! They were both strangers here. Where would she be heading? Either the bus station or a train station was Casey's guess.

Whoa... a police car double-parked just up the street! She ran toward it and was only steps away when she had second thoughts. She didn't want to involve the police. If the authorities knew Debra tried evading the law again, it would just add to her list of charges.

"Did you see that girl?" the cop behind the wheel asked his partner, reentering the car with a couple cups of coffee.

"She's still on the run, up the street."

"She was heading straight for me, and then veered off."

"Curious enough to see where she's going?"

"I think so." He edged back into the left lane when it was clear in both directions and made a U turn in the middle of the block.

Meanwhile, Casey had stopped a middle-aged man in a suit who looked intelligent, and asked "Can you direct me to the bus station?"

He paused for a minute, "The bus station... It's quite a ways... it's about, I don't know, 10 or 12 blocks that way, and another few blocks down Jefferson, I think."

"How about the train station?"

"The train station?" He was stumped, "I don't know where the train station is."

"Thanks, guv'nor," she sputtered, speeding on her way. Then she slowed to a brisk walk. 10 or 12 blocks, then more blocks. She couldn't run all the way. But Debra couldn't either. Unless she took a cab. Casey would take a cab. She cut into the gutter, between parked cars, and waited for an opportunity to cross the street.

She started hailing passing cabs. Conscious of nothing else, she didn't even notice the police car that had darted into an open parking space not far behind her. Soon she was in a bright yellow cab, on the way to the bus station. Even if Debra got there several minutes before her, the chances of any bus pulling out immediately with her on it were slim. Casey calmed down enough to think straight, and she felt a lot more optimistic about catching Debra before the little devil doll managed to get away.

Chapter 56

A real man handles the situation

THE CAB COMPANY HAD BEEN their first call. James Ames had come along as driver and companion, just to add his support to Robert's missions. Convincing the manager that all costs would be taken care of was all he was concerned about. After a short discussion and another exchange of identification, they were assured there would be no charges against Leno or Miss Lavish.

Ames had waited until mid-morning to call Esther Williams, hoping her less than agreeable husband Fernando Lamas would be off at work. Lamas was doing more directing of TV dramas than acting, Ames knew, and a little matter like the cab dunking at home wasn't enough of an excuse to ignore his studio responsibilities.

Now they were at her door. She opened it with a bright smile, which put them both at ease immediately. She offered them coffee, and when they were comfortably seated in her modest living room, Robert gave her a brief and only partially fictitious explanation of the circumstances leading up to the dramatic events of the day before. All costs to her for repair of the pool and any other damage to the property would be paid by Robert, acting on behalf of the Galactic Publishing Company of New York. Matter closed. There would be no charges against Debra, poor girl, a confused young lady with so many problems. More of a victim than a villain, surely.

"Your amazing rescue of the young lady should be known by the public," Ames led into a slight change of subject. He obviously had something else on his mind. "If you agree, I could see to it that a news report made it to the press."

Esther was still smiling, but her head was nodding no. "I'd rather it wasn't reported at all, Mr. Ames. My husband wouldn't like it."

"But it's such an uplifting story. Movie heroine a heroine in real life." The modest agent was doing more selling on this matter than he usually put forward on a million dollar contract negotiation, and Robert wondered why it mattered to him at all.

Esther would hear none of it, and stood up to indicate she considered the meeting closed. She escorted them to the door, ever smiling, charming to the last farewell.

"What do you think of her?" Ames asked Robert as they started back to the city.

"Very natural and unaffected for a movie star, I'd say" was Robert's assessment.

"She's more complicated than she appears." Ames seemed eager to reveal a few not so secret rumors he'd picked up through his insider occupation. "She has another home, closeby, where her underage children live with a fulltime nanny/housekeeper."

"That is a little unusual, I guess," Robert didn't find it very startling though.

"She's been married twice before, but now she's a sex slave to Lamas. Gave up her career completely. She's past the pin-up movie star years, but I could keep her in the public eye and making a fortune on TV and franchise deals if she'd go along with the program."

So that was it. He was a natural born agent after all, just a little more sedate than most, but alert to representing hot personalities. Robert wasn't very interested in Ames' plots, but the man had sparked his curiosity.

"Why do you say she's a sex slave?" The idea was absurdly alien to him.

"Lamas won't live with kids, as a family man. So she's given up her children, her career, everything, to satisfy that guy's every selfish wish, every whim. And he's an arrogant son-of-a-bitch!"

What passion Ames was displaying! So out of character for him, Robert thought, though he was basing his observation on a very short acquaintance. He decided to change the subject before he learned a lot more than he cared to about the suddenly loquacious show business agent.

"Have you ever met Marlon Brando?" he asked, "I've heard he's a genius, and then I've also heard he's a moron."

"Brando. Oh, yeah, I know plenty about Brando." He'd supplied the perfect name to start Ames on a novel length, unexpurgated, back alley biography...

Chapter 57

Catfight between heroine and harridan

T HE MAIN GREYHOUND BUS STATION in central Los Angeles was one big jumble of suitcases and hot dogs and umbrellas and every kind of esoteric junk, not to mention people of all ages, sizes and nationalities, but apparently, after Casey's initial search, no Debra.

It was impossible to steer a straight course through the crowd, but she looked everywhere, all the side rooms, the toilets, the lockers, every corner of the place, and then she went out to the bus docks and scouted there too.

No trace of Debra.

She hurried to the ticket counter and waited impatiently in the shortest line for the family ahead of her to complete their business.

"Have you sold a ticket in the last ten minutes to a pretty young blonde woman?" she asked the clerk, a bit breathlessly, having been almost at a steady trot for at least that long.

He looked at her with the impassive expression of a man who'd heard every idiotic question imaginable after years of confronting a steady stream of fellow citizens daily for years.

"Did she have a big blue nose?"

"A blue nose... No, she doesn't have a blue nose." At first Casey didn't realize he was putting her on.

"Well, that's the only blonde I remember, the one with the blue nose."

She stepped away, suddenly aware of how silly her question was. There was no other way to describe Debra, but it fit half the young women in the city, and she didn't even know what kind of outfit she'd walked out of the store wearing.

She felt deflated, but rallied to study the arrivals and departures board. The most likely of interest to Debra, Casey guessed, was a bus headed for Arizona, leaving in about ten minutes.

There wasn't any point in trying to find the girl anywhere else. She found a seat in a corner spot where she could see the whole interior of the building and a good deal of the outside platforms as well. If Debra didn't show up for that bus heading west, Casey knew she'd lost her.

The minutes passed slowly, as they always do when all you've got to do is watch and wait, but finally the loudspeaker announced the Arizona destinations, and almost immediately Debra strolled into view, through a side door, heading straight for the boarding gate.

Casey jumped to her feet, scrambled through another door leading outside, and was just in time to grab Debra's wrist as she placed one foot on the steps inside the door of the bus!

She pulled her out, almost knocking the girl off her feet, but Debra regained her balance and threw a hand, not quite a fist, in Casey's direction.

The sure-to-be serious catfight was brought up short as a stern looking policeman put himself between them, and grabbed an arm of each in vise-like grips.

Both girls wilted instantly, and all offensive intent evaporated as the officer pulled them away from the bus and the wide eyes of the others in line.

"What's the problem with you two?" he inquired politely.

When there was no answer, he decided a subtle threat might be persuasive. Without loosening his hold on them, his tone was quiet but cold. "You've both been acting strange, and it looked like you were about to come to blows."

He looked straight at Casey, "So far, all we've got on you is stalking and assault..."

"Oh, blimey! Assault! Please, officer, it's nothing like that!"

"English, eh? What is it, then?"

"We're friends. Aren't we, Debra."

"Sure. We're friends." Debra didn't give him a bit of a smile, which didn't help.

"She stole my dress." Casey blurted, not able to think of anything else on the spur of the moment.

"Did you steal your friend's dress?" the officer was apparently prepared to accept that, as a beginning at least.

"No," Debra sulked.

"I guess I'll have to arrest you both," he decided, "Come along."

"Hold on, Mr. policeman," Casey balked, "We were just horsing around. It was hide and seek. We were playing a game."

"That's right," Debra finally remembered the power of her smile, "We were just goofing."

Her charm was still effective, and seemed to turn the tide. He loosened his hold without disengaging completely, and gave them a long look.

"You two are a little too old for hide and seek, aren't you?"

Casey put her arm around Debra, and they both smiled. "We didn't mean to cause a scene, really we didn't." The two of them, operating together, were irresistible.

"My partner and I have been watching you both for the last half hour, and we just had to see what would happen when you got together."

"Where's your partner?"

"He's cruising around the neighborhood. We're supposed to keep things peaceful and orderly, but you didn't look that dangerous, so I figured, whatever it was, I could handle it."

"It's over. No more games. Right, Debra?"

"We'll be good, officer," Debra assured him. She'd decided there was no percentage in having additional trouble with the authorities.

Chapter 58

Old-fashioned punishment applied

H IS PLAN TO RELAX FOR awhile before their sure-to-be tense dinner with Astaire and who knows how many others that evening was stymied by the reception Robert received at the hotel when he got back to check on Casey and Debra.

"This bitch is treating me like a criminal!" Debra squawked, "She's been abusing me!" Casey had managed to prove she was stronger and able to dominate Debra, which the girl considered abuse.

"She ran out on me," Casey explained calmly. "I had to track her down at the bus station. She had a ticket to the border of Mexico."

"Tucson, Arizona isn't the border of Mexico," Debra sniffled into a tissue.

Robert took a long look at her, all the while comparing all those idealistic pictures in his memory with the soggy, sullen character she appeared to be at the moment. She was dressed prettily in a nice yellow dress, and her hair was neatly coiffed, but he examined her perfect features with a more critical eye than he ever had before.

"Tucson isn't Mexico, but it isn't California either, and you were prohibited from leaving the state."

"Phooey! I'll go where I want to!"

"I made myself responsible for you, Debra. Do you realize the situation I'd be in if you ran out on me?"

"It was your idea, not mine! I'm not going to stay here another day! You can't make me!"

It was such an irrational outburst that Robert had no alternative. He grabbed her, threw her over his lap and beat her bottom as hard as he could until her howls filled the room and his hand was stinging so bad he had to stop.

Then came a cascade of tears as she sprawled on the floor, resting on a hip. not her blistered buttocks. Only a light summer dress and a thin pair of silk panties had come between herself and his heavy hand, so the throbbing pain was sure to last long enough to make a lasting impression, along with the memory of maidenly humiliation. But she wasn't seriously bruised.

"I'm sorry you had to see that," Robert remarked to Casey, a predictable statement from a man who had only witnessed such spectacles himself in old movies on TV, after which the perpetrator, somebody like Jimmy Cagney, would deliver the exact inane dialogue he'd just expressed to his gentler partner.

"If you hadn't done it, I'd have to," she slapped her thigh, unable to restrain the broad grin on her face. There was no socially correct spin to put on it, the girl was acting like a child and had to be disciplined like one.

"You're a spoiled brat, Debra," Robert addressed the sobbing miscreant, "Apparently we'll have to treat you like prisoner until the authorities decide what legal punishment you deserve."

"I want to call my father," she whimpered.

"You can call your father, but in my presence. Any lies you tell him will be contradicted by me, so you might as well tell him the truth and hope he's got more patience with you than I have."

After she'd gained her composure, Debra put in a call to her parents in Connecticut. She didn't lie, but the story she gave them was so convoluted, it scarcely made sense. Apparently he agreed not to restrict her use of his credit card, which was her main concern when she finally realized she was stuck with the full consequences of her misguided Hollywood adventure.

By the time James Ames arrived to drive them to Astaire's residence, all three had spruced up adequately to attend a dignified dinner. They'd done a little more shopping, and Robert had his suit dry cleaned and pressed. Debra picked up a pair of high heels and a short jacket to match the yellow dress, and a pair of earrings. Casey stuck with low heels, just in case she had to do any more running after her unpredictable gal pal that evening, but she did buy a very neat belt that went well with her slacks, and a colorful scarf. She remembered that Astaire seemed to like scarves. Robert thought she was quite a dish in the outfit, but he didn't make a comment. His admiration of Debra's looks had forever soured, he knew, now that her under the surface ugly personality had come to the fore so formidably.

Chapter 59

Dinner with Fred Astaire

T HIS IS JUST AN INFORMAL family dinner," Astaire tried to reassure everyone, but he knew the attendant butler, the maid with a succession of courses, the fine dining service and candle-lit table would give it an aura of importance.

Arthur was in fine form, maintaining as impassive a countenance as ever he'd achieved on screen, quick to refill any half empty wine glass. The maid was a little giggly, but efficient enough. Astaire was in formal fettle, despite his disclaimer to any gravity attached to the gathering. Flossie was stonily silent after a cordial greeting as she arrived last at the table, having skipped the cocktails in the study. It was probably for the best because that was where Astaire had remarked on the attractive charms of both young ladies in attendance, and in particular what a remarkable transformation Debra had managed. His mother might not have been able to withhold making a comment if she'd been within earshot of those particular compliments. She'd been appalled when advised the girl had been invited to her home after trespassing so flagrantly the day before, but promised not to make any fuss about it when the guests were assembled. Astaire was confident the wine at dinner would put her in a genial mood, and forestall any complaint from the old lady.

He was obligated to include Debra in the party when advised by Mr. Ames of her uncertain but somehow pertinent relationship with Mr. Trabur, and the fact that both he and Astaire were responsible for her whereabouts for the foreseeable future. It would not have been smart to leave her alone somewhere with both Robert and Casey out of her sight.

Debra, to her credit, had recovered from Robert's caveman rebuke, and warmed to the occasion, reveling in the company of a genuine Hollywood legend, even though she'd never actually seen any of his movies. Her movie heroes populated a more recent generation.

She listed her credits, which, not surprising, hardly impressed anyone. Then she spoke of her aspirations, which were even less interesting or unusual.

Flossie told a joke that was probably a bit risqué when she first heard it a half century before, which was so silly from the mouth of a woman her age that everyone had a big laugh.

They could hear a phone ringing in another room, and a few moments later, Arthur returned to announce, "A call for you, sir. It's Mickey Rooney."

"Oh." Astaire debated with himself for a second, "Okay, I'll take it."

Arthur retrieved a phone from nearby, and brought it to the table. They could only hear one side of the conversation, of course.

"Hello. Hello, Mickey. Uh huh. Okay. Yeah. No. Yeah. No. I don't think so. No. I'll think about it. Okay. Yeah. Goodbye, Mickey."

He handed the phone back to Arthur, looked a bit dazed for a minute, shook his head and refocused on his guests.

"Mickey Rooney," he muttered, but took a mouthful of broccoli buds without commenting further about the call. Robert couldn't help wondering if they were friends too or whether it had been an unexpected call from a stranger. He was beginning to suspect celebrities lead even more unusual lives than he had imagined.

Astaire seemed curious about Casey, and drew her out more than she usually was in company or, for that matter, with just one other person. She revealed a lot more about her history than Robert had ever heard from her, and both men were especially fascinated when she told them about her riding, and familiarity with horse racing and training horses.

Astaire seemed particularly interested in the unhappy circumstances that led to her long separation from her father, old Thimble, Astaire's track buddy.

Robert and Ames each summed up their lives in one sentence summaries, which was just enough.

Over desert, their host finally brought up the matter that had brought them together.

"Kelly dropped by this morning." he addressed Ames, "he was very persuasive. He thinks I should okay the release of this film you've discovered, Mr. Trabur." He turned his attention to Robert, then paused for dramatic effect.

"I've thought it over from every angle." he addressed nobody in particular, his hands clasped together almost as if he was in prayer, looking up above their heads to the ceiling beyond, "I can't approve it," he declared with finality. "I just can't allow it to be released."

The silence was so loud, he added a soft "I'm sorry."

Flossie was the first to push her chair back and get to her feet. "Goodnight, everyone," she said simply, and made her way out of the dining room toward the main staircase. Her son had suggested they install an elevator but she'd nixed the idea. Going up and down those stairs was her exercise, and she was determined to stay active to her last breath.

"A fine lady, your mother," Robert said.

"Indeed. And a good joke teller." Ames got his own laugh with that remark.

"Coffee will be served in the library," Arthur announced.

Chapter 60

Jessie and Mortimer on a date

JESSIE MATTHEWS LOOKED PRETTY HOT for an old vaudeville pony. She checked herself out in the full length mirror next to her bathroom door. Scoop necked pink dress to show plenty of her ample bosom, short skirted to show plenty of leg, still as shapely as ever, wide belt to hold in her waist, expanding annually despite butterless toast for breakfast, dry salad for lunch and naked fish with celery for dinner, five days a week. Mortimer Poundstack was due to arrive any minute to pick her up for dinner at Maxim's and dancing at the new disco club in Piccadilly. Mort wouldn't be dancing, but there was always someone who knew her and would ask her to dance when she went out in public, as often as she pleased. Well, almost always. Fleeting fame, the curse of the stage.

She surveyed the living room one last time. It too was shipshape, the only room in the house that was, the only room in the house visitors ever saw. After two disastrous marriages and a good number of passionate romances, Jessie was leading a celibate life, an independent, stress free life after severe enough despondencey to put her in a mental hospital for many months.

But she was still attractive enough, and flirtatious enough to enjoy the attention of the male sex. Lately the most ardent of her admirers was the distinguished Mortimer Poundstack, a man of considerable wealth and stature in London society. She had politely declined his offer of marriage, but he was patient, confident she would eventually accept, and they enjoyed each other's company.

At precisely seven PM, her doorbell announced his arrival. Max, his chauffer, would remain in the limousine until they were ready to leave.

"Hello Mort," she greeted him with a kiss on the cheek.

"Hello darling." he tossed his top hat on a chair and made his way to the bar as if he were entering his own home. "Did you remember to get some ice today?"

"I did. It's one American custom I approve... ice in all the drinks, even soft drinks."

He mixed them, knowing her choice as well as his own, as she arranged herself decorously on the couch. They were a comfortable pair, beyond the early stages of a relationship, at the point where each knew the liberties they could take and the boundaries beyond which they mustn't cross.

"I got a long distance phone call today, from California, from Fred Astaire."

He handed her the light vodka and orange juice blend she liked, and took a seat beside her.

"Well, what did he have to say?"

"He said no, we couldn't release it, here or there"

"You're smiling. You don't appear to be in the least disappointed."

"I'm not. He was very complimentary. He told me I was delightful in the film, that he wanted to go ahead with it but his agent strongly objected."

"He could overrule his agent, surely."

"I'm sure he could, but the agent said he was only a supporting player, ten percent of the picture, and I overshadowed him."

"I suppose his ego couldn't tolerate that," Poundstack scoffed.

"He said that if I wanted to pursue it," Jessie continued, "his part would have to be eliminated entirely, and new footage of another actor put in his place."

"I don't see how that could be done."

"It probably could, but why bother? I'm perfectly content to keep it a private little movie of my own, just a souvenir of meeting Mr. Astaire, the greatest musical star of the century." she was sincere in that observation, just as much a fan of his as any ordinary Astaire admirer anywhere in the world where his movies had been distributed.

"Well, that's that then."

"He was very nice," she was in a very luxurious mood, recalling everything he had said, every compliment, every phrase of praise he heaped upon her. For a little while she was back at the top of the heap, the belle of the ball, a countrywide sensation. The glitter had very gradually fallen away over the years, and Jessie had adjusted to her dimished fame a lot easier than she had adjusted to the ordinary hassles of real life, real relationships, advancing age.

"Did he mention anything about Casey?"

"He said he'd had dinner with her and Mr. Trabur the night before but couldn't call then because of the time difference. It was the middle of the night here. He mentioned it was a coincidence that he knew Casey's father. Small world, huh?"

Poundstack did a doubletake worthy of a Mack Sennet silent star. "He knew Casey's father? How did that come up? How did he know she *had* a father?"

"I don't know, Mort," Jessie snapped out of her reverie. "That's all he said... he knew her father."

Their evening went as planned, but he couldn't stop thinking about that remark.

Chapter 61

Fast farewells from slow growing friends

THE DAYS PASSED SLOWLY FOR Robert and Casey. Now that they each had a more friendly attitude toward the other, it seemed there were so many distractions, they never got an opportunity to sit down for a quiet conversation. They had to take turns watching Debra, who didn't give them a lot of trouble except for her constant whining and complaining. Robert had to exchange several phone call with Mr. Fingerroth, his boss, the Galactic publisher who was not very happy about the mounting expenses and disappointing results of Robert's canceled Jessie Matthews project. They spent considerable time, at long distance rates, trying to figure out a way to make something out of it.

Robert called Jessie a day after Astaire talked to her. They'd decided the bad news should be delivered first by Astaire himself rather than Robert. She took it well, to the relief of them both. She thanked Robert for his efforts and wished him well and told him he was always welcome to visit her again if he ever got back to England. He asked her if she'd yet received the package he'd mailed a few days earlier. She hadn't, but would watch for it.

Debra's court date came up sooner than expected, only three days after the incident at the pool. It was a simple affair, just one of several minor cases presented to a harried looking judge with a frown frozen in concrete in a large courtroom filled with litigants, witnesses, lawyers and a few idle crime story regulars who, having nothing else to do, were entertained hearing the details of their community's misdemeanors. The latter were well known by the court staff, evicted when the room filled over the city ordinance capacity. Casey didn't join them, but James Ames went along with Robert as a character witness. The judge heard the arresting officer's report and, burdened with a full roster that day, didn't ask for anything additional from any of them, even Debra. She obviously looked so young, innocent and terrified that ten years at hard labor would have been excessive. He gave her a short lecture, fined her $300, told her where to pay it, and dismissed her. Debra had to remain another day, while Robert got the total repair figures from the cab company and Esther Williams. Her father's credit card took a couple of major hits that day, but when they parted the next morning, she was as cheerful as if nothing unusual at all had transpired.

Casey wrote a letter to Mortimer Poundstack, telling him she couldn't come back right away. She didn't mention anything about her father, but she'd seen him several times, visited him at his home, and was so angry with Poundstack that she didn't really want to go back to him at all! Thimble had explained how he'd been forced out of Casey's life, sent out of the country so there would never be any contact between them.

Then, as soon as Debra was gone, so was Robert. He had to get back to work. Saying goodbye to Casey was tough. They'd gone through a lot together in just a few days, and he didn't even have an opportunity to tell her how much he admired her pluck and loyalty. She felt the same unresolved disappointment, that she hadn't had the opportunity to tell him she was sorry for the unfriendly way she'd acted during the first part of their adventure together.

But the clock never stops, they'd said goodbye, and now he was gone. She sat alone in the hotel room James Ames had found for them and knew she had nowhere to go except back home to her uncle.

Robert had called Ames to thank him for all his help, and say goodbye.

Ames had called Astaire to tell him Robert had left, and Astaire called Casey to invite her and her father to dinner.

Casey and her father to Astaire's for another dinner? Was this famous man so desperate for company? It seemed ridiculous, but she accepted, of course.

Arrangements were made. Arthur would call for them in the limousine on the day following the surprise invitation. Casey would have another day to explore Los Angeles, and naturally she'd need a different ensemble than the one she'd worn before. This time, now that she wouldn't be compared with the always smartly styled Debra, she'd wear a dress.

Chapter 62

Shlug Mugger gets a reprimand

SHLUG MUGGER WAS GOING ABOUT his business at the stables when he suddenly realized his employer was standing at the side of the corral, dressed for riding. Tapping his riding crop against his leg, grimly glowering with the expression of a man about to explode, he didn't otherwise move or say a word.

"Do you want to go for a ride, Mr. Poundstack?" Shlug greeted him respectfully, changing direction in midstride to approach, wondering what was on the old man's mind. Normally he'd have called to arrange for a horse to be saddled and ready when he arrived.

"You notified Casey's father that she was going to America, didn't you," he accused Shlug with icy anger in every syllable.

He hesitated a moment, but knew it would be futile to deny it. "Yes, I did."

"I should thrash you right now, and throw you out!" He slapped his whip against the side of his boot more vigorously, clearly conveying his barely contained fury.

Shlug didn't say a word. He faced the old man with a direct gaze of his own. He wasn't ashamed of what he'd done, or in a mood to apologize.

"You betrayed me!" There was no need for either of them to bring up everything Poundstack had done for Shlug over the years. Like Casey, he'd taken the orphaned son of an old employee into his care when he was a teenager, and found a place for him at the stables.

"Saddle two horses. You'll ride with me." He didn't want anyone else to overhear what he had to say to the young man.

There was a horse trail along the outer borders of Poundstack's property which went all around three sides, following the fence line, which at a slow walk would take almost a half hour. As soon as they got underway, Poundstack got right to the point.

"I understand you're Casey's best mate, and you were pals with Dingle too, when you were a mere lad, so I can understand why you did it. But I got a phone call from Casey. Her mission has been accomplished, but she's stalling about when she's going to return home. She might not return home at all, and it's **your fault** if she doesn't!"

Shlug still couldn't think of anything to say, but he was mortified. That certainly wasn't his wish. He missed Casey, and the thought of never seeing her again was like a knife thrust into his heart.

"As if I didn't have anything else to worry about..." Poundstack spit out the wad of saliva he'd worked up already, lecturing his wayward ward.

"I'm sorry, Mr. Poundstack," was Shlug's feeble apology. He hadn't realized the possible consequences of his actions. The horses ambled along without any guidance from their riders, following the trail they always followed on exactly the same route.

"She said she was sending me a letter. I haven't received it yet, and I don't know what it says, but I suspect it's going to be, well..."

"Casey loves her life here, Mr. Poundstack. She wouldn't just leave suddenly like that."

"When that letter arrives, you're going to write her back right away."

"Anything you say, Mr. Poundstack," Shlug meant it sincerely.

"Exactly," he went on, "I'll tell you what to say, and you'll put it in your words. We'll write a letter together."

They passed through a grove of trees. A branch had fallen across the trail, evidence of a recent heavy rainstorm, and both horses were so used to staying on the trail that they just stopped rather than go around it.

By the time they got back to the stables, Poundstack's anger had cooled. He liked Shlug, and realized he probably would have done precisely the same thing in the boy's place.

"Are you going to think first before you stick your nose in my business again?" he demanded to know, as they dismounted.

"Yes sir," Slug said, "I will. I surely will."

Chapter 63

Not phone sex, just phone petting

CASEY ENJOYED GETTING TO KNOW her father, but it soon became obvious to her that he had a routine of his own, and there was really no place for her now, a grown woman, in his life. Not on a permanent basis. She'd sent a serious letter to her uncle, an angry letter, but she hadn't actually threatened not to return. What else could she do? Maybe Robert could advise her. On a whim, she dialed his office number in Manhattan.

"Hello, Casey," he said when they were connected, "I've been thinking about you."

She liked hearing that, and after a few exchanges about the weather and the latest headline stories on the news, she got to the purpose of her call.

In a flood she gave him the shorthand explanation of how her uncle had manipulated the lives of her parents and herself, and she didn't know how she felt about returning to him.

"Well, why don't you come here for a couple weeks. You can think it over, and—"

"Go back to New York? I don't know..." She really hadn't expected an invitation like that.

"Sure," Robert was rapidly warming to the idea, "You haven't had much chance to experience anything positive in my country, and who knows when you'll get back again. We could see a show, maybe, and—"

"Thanks, Robert," she could tell he was running low on ideas right off the cuff, "I'll think about it. You've cheered me up, anyway."

"Seriously. The more I think about it, the more certain I am it would be the best thing for you to do until you can decide just where you want to go from here."

"Goodbye, Robert," she said, suddenly feeling a little embarrassed. Had she spoken too personally with him? They hadn't exchanged much more than name, age and serial numbers up to this point in their relationship, and now she was confiding her most intimate feelings. Had she been too forward with the man? No. It was all his idea. She wouldn't go, of course. But at least the tears had stopped flowing.

Chapter 64

The cryptic call to Poundstack

"A call for you, sir. He wouldn't give his name. He said he had the film, that you'd know what he means." Cummings had entered so silently, Poundstack's first awareness of his butler's presence was his voice, delivering that message. He was at his desk, writing checks, a dreaded regular duty he had to perform personally.

He didn't know what it meant, but he picked up the phone anyway.

"This is Mortimer Poundstack."

"You don't know me, but I know you're a friend of Jessie Matthews."

Suddenly he did know what it was about. "That's right."

"I've got the film."

"And..." Poundstack knew what was coming next.

"I know everything. I want a thousand pounds for the film. If you won't pay, I'll send the film to the BBC." A man of few words, he'd chosen them carefully.

"Well... just what do you think the BBC will do with it?"

"They'll show it on TV, of course."

"No they won't. I'll call them immediately after I hang up. I'll tell them it's my property, and if they show it, I'll sue them."

"You're probably right," it was an unusual response from a man demanding ransom, but he could think on his feet, and came up with an alternative, "Maybe I'll send it to one of the networks in the USA. So you'll have to call all of them and tell them what might be turning up... which means a lot of people will know it exists."

Poundstack didn't bother to reply. He knew his caller didn't need any prompting.

"If a lot of people know it exists, there's no way it will stay out of circulation. You know that as well as I do."

Poundstack did. If it were released, no matter what excuses Jessie made, Astaire would blame her, and who knows what punishment she'd be in for. By the end of the call, he agreed to pay the man a thousand pounds.

Chapter 65

An encore dinner at the star's estate

"You look lovely this evening, Miss Thimble", Astaire said with a big smile, as they found their seats around his table. He'd already told his other lady guest how lovely she was, before the others arrived.

"And you're a grand poopentate, Mr. Astaire, to invite an old horse radish like me to dinner," Thimble said, taking a seat next to his daughter.

"How about me, Fred," Irving Berlin piped up, "Am I lovely too?"

"You're as lovely as an old shoe, Irving." Astaire grinned, "But I love you anyway."

Astaire's only other guest for the evening was a tiny middle-aged woman of about fifty he called V.E., his nickname for her, who seemed quite mysterious to Casey. When she smiled or laughed, which was seldom, she seemed twenty years younger, but when she was not part of the conversation, her thoughts inner directed, she appeared just as much older than her years.

V. E. laughed as Berlin started softly singing ad lib lyrics about an old shoe, and Casey was relieved to see that. She'd appeared rather sad when introduced, and since Casey had no idea who she was, it made her uneasy.

"Where's Arthur," Flossie demanded to know. "Here we are, and he's not."

"Arthur." Astaire called out in a loud voice.

The butler came rushing in from the kitchen. "Sorry, sir," was all he said, offering no excuse for his tardy arrival.

Millie, the maid, followed him, pushing a serving cart, with several pitchers on top, which Arthur used to fill everyone's glasses with the beverage of their choice.

When she returned a few minutes later, with plates individually prepared, restaurant style, with the evening's main course, Arthur leaned over to address the host in a half whisper:

"There's a bit of a problem, sir. Cook substituted another vegetable. But there are no potatoes."

"No potatoes?" Astaire seemed incredulous.

"What's that?" Flossie, at the other end of the table, had very good hearing. "No potatoes? Why aren't there any potatoes, Arthur? Didn't you drive cook to market this morning?"

"I did, Madam, but she didn't remember to get potatoes."

"What are we supposed to put our gravy on... the peas?" Flossie was clearly flummoxed. The gravy had been served separately in a fancy tureen, so everybody could use whatever amount they wished.

"I like peas with gravy," Berlin asserted.

"I never eat potatoes," V.E. piped up, "except potato chips."

"We've got plenty of bread, mother." her boy Freddie tried to soothe her, "We can make hot roast beef sandwiches, the way they serve it in diners."

"Cook's been crying, sir," Arthur confided solemnly. "She's very upset."

"Tell cook there's no problem. It looks like a fine roast beef dinner."

"Thank you, sir."

After a few bites, they all agreed it was a marvelous meal.

"The cook's husband, Tony, is our groundskeeper," their host explained. "He usually picks up a big fifty pound sack of potatoes at the Farmer's Market every month or so, but he's been in the hospital for several weeks with a severe case of shingles."

"Saint's mercy." Dingle exclaimed, "Even a mild case of shingles is enough misery for any poor soul."

"Horses get shingles, too," Casey added, "Our vet told me..." She decided not to expand on her one experience back home. Not her experience, but the experience of a horse in her care.

"The yard looks terrible," if Flossie couldn't complain anymore about the potatoes, she was determined to complain about something else.

"The doctor told me Tony is improving, mother," Astaire gently informed her, "He should be back home in just a few days."

"When weeds are overrunning our entire property, it just encourages trespassers to jump the fence and tromp all over."

"Oh, mother, please..."

"Arthur has plenty of spare time," she insisted, "He could mow the lawn."

"Arthur is our inside man. He doesn't work outside." His tone had the weight of finality on the subject.

The rest of the meal went smoothly, after the crisis concerning the potatoes had passed, despite the varied personalities in attendance. Astaire thought bringing Dingle Thimble in contact with Irving Berlin would be amusing for the songwriter. Thimble spewed out such colorful British expressions that Astaire knew his old pal would take note and possibly use some of them in the lyrics of a new song.

He only invited Vera Ellen, a dear friend, a costar from an earlier decade, when he knew she knew the other guests or if they were civilians like Casey and her father, not movie people who would know her circumstances and be uncomfortable. Once on top of the world, Vera Ellen's career had come to a dead stop ten years before. Her second marriage had failed, and her only child, a daughter, had died while an infant just six years earlier. The Thimbles didn't know any of this, and she did seem more cheerful as the evening went on. She'd been so lively as a youngster, and could still light up a small room with her dormant personality among non-threatening company upon casual occasions like this.

"I'm thinking about going to the track next weekend, Dingle," Astaire said between a forkful of lettuce and a sip of Pepsi Cola, his drink of choice, "Your track. Santa Anita. What do you say we go together and put down a few bets?"

"I'd be rightly honored, Mr. A," Thimble replied, with a twinkle in his eye, "We'll sort out the flash from the fizzle."

Astaire winked at Berlin, who just smiled.

During a lull in the conversation, Astaire made a comment out of the blue. Laying his fork down, he wiped his lips with his napkin and addressed her directly. "You know. V.E., of all the girls I danced with, I had a harder time keeping up with you than any of the others."

She almost lost a mouthful of gravy-free peas. "Horsefeathers," she said. "Horsefeathers and elephant wings!"

"No, it's true. Did I ever tell you that before?"

"You probably told them all some kind of blarney. All of your dancing partners!"

"You did some spins so fast in one number I don't think the camera could catch it. If they isolated the frames, you'd be facing front in one to facing back in the very next one."

"I could spin fast because I was so skinny. I didn't have all those curvy parts, like Rita Hayworth, to carry around."

"Oh, was that it?" Astaire teased, "I knew there had to be some explanation."

He managed to get a big smile out of her, and told another backstage story from their one picture together. He'd gotten along with all of his leading ladies, which is why he always declined to name his favorite. His favorite was the one he was with when they asked.

"You probably won't believe me either," Berlin mumbled, just loud enough to be heard, "but you were sort of the inspiration, well, you were the inspiration for a song I wrote after watching 'The Belle of New York'."

They all waited for the rest of his recollection, but he seemed disinclined to say anything more about it.

"What song was that, Irving?" Astaire asked his timid friend.

"It was called 'Spin Like a Top'."

"See," Astaire seemed to bounce a few inches out of his chair, "Irving wrote a song about you!"

"I don't believe it," Vera Ellen said, "I never heard of a song called 'Spin Like a Top."

"I didn't say it was ever published. I wrote a lot of songs that were never published."

"How did it go, Irving?" Astaire coaxed, but to no avail.

"I don't remember. I only remember the title. If I didn't have a list of songs I wrote, I wouldn't remember more than a few now. Most of them were lousy."

His comment was so matter-of-fact, so undemonstrative, that they all laughed.

As the chuckles subsided, they heard the phone ringing in another room. When Arthur next appeared to refill their wine and water and other beverage glasses, his master gave him an anxious look.

"Was it her again?" his jaw clenched in suspense. Whoever it was, he was hoping it wasn't her.

"It was for me, sir," Arthur informed him.

"For you." Astaire furrowed a brow slightly, not extremely, just moderately, "You've been getting a number of calls recently, Arthur. What's going on? Am I losing you?"

"I'm considering an offer to franchise my name, sir, which is as surprising to me as it must be to you."

"Franchise your name? It sounds intriguing. I franchised my name once. For a chain of dancing academys. Took me years to get my name erased from those places."

"I think it was Mery Griffin's idea. He's always coming up with goofy ideas."

"Be careful. Don't sign anything until you know exactly what the deal is. top to bottom."

"What do they want with your name, Arthur?" Irving Berlin, who was often in the house, considered the proper but cordial butler a personal friend.

"Apparently it's for a chain of fish and chips restaurants." He said with a straight face, so they believed it must be true.

"Like McDonald's and Long John Silver's?" Vera Ellen joined the conversation.

"Seems pretty far-fetched to me," Arthur deadpanned, "But they're offering me a considerable amount of money."

"Well, I'll have my lawyer look at the contract," Astaire offered, "If you want me to. No charge." He volunteered free service from his lawyer, which was a rather imperious assumption, even for him.

"Thank you, sir, but I consider myself fairly proficient at negotiating contracts. I never had an agent or anyone to handle my business affairs, and had many contracts to attend to over the years." He carried the beverage pitchers back to the kitchen without a backward glance.

"Was that a putdown?" Astaire asked, going from face to face.

"I don't think so, Fred," Berlin assured his sensitive host.

"Arthur puts a sarcastic edge to everything he says," Flossie spoke up, as she often did whenever she sensed any sign of apprehension in a group... or a private conversation with one other person, for that matter. "He's a snob. Which is a good trait in a butler."

"Arthur is a good man," Berlin was adamant.

"Arthur is a very good man," Astaire agreed.

"E plays a straight bat for an old silver top," was Thimble's comment.

Nobody knew what it meant, but Vera Ellen let out the loudest laugh of them all.

Chapter 66

Shlug Mugger takes charge

THE ARRANGEMENTS FOR THE RANSOM transfer were as complex as if it were a million bags of gold for the High Maharajah's virgin princess bride, but to Mortimer Poundstack, a thousand pounds was a mere pittance in exchange for the Matthews film. He wondered initially why the caller hadn't demanded more, which led to the obvious conclusion. If he decided to call the man's bluff, there was really no alternative. No reputable distributer would handle such a property without legal authorization, and no disreputable distributer could hope to find buyers, so they wouldn't pay for it either.

The smalltime grifter, whoever he was, made a modest demand, figuring it would be insignificant enough that Poundstack would pay it just to nullify the nuisance.

It wasn't the money, it was just the principle of the thing. The crusty old curmudgeon was determined he wouldn't get away with it!

Shlug Mugger, dressed inconspicuously as a no class youth, common everywhere in the city, was Poundstack's companion as Max drove them to the London pub where he was to wait until contacted. It was Shlug who suggested that probably wouldn't be the end of it, that Poundstack would probably get a phone call there or a message would be slipped to him, directing him to a second location. They worked out a plan to foil whatever nefarious scheme had been devised by the perpetrator, who, both of them agreed, was most likely working alone, without accomplices.

There was a low fog hanging over every London district on the evening they set out for the switch, and a solemn silence muffled the normal sounds of the city after dark. Traffic flowed slower than on a clear moonlit night, everyone cautious, knowing how quickly another vehicle can appear out of nowhere.

Shlug was set to enter the Royal Dungeon, a low dive on a scraggly street near the center of the city, alone, an hour before Poundstack was scheduled to arrive, and nurse a beer, watching for any suspicious activity, then join his boss to topple the villain if he did actually appear there, or follow his nibs to the second location, if that was necessary. Shlug carried a short sturdy club in his loose trousers, which, if applied with force behind a man's knees, was guaranteed to put anyone down on the floor, no matter how big or fearsome.

After entering, the cocky jockey ordered a mug of draft beer at the bar, then made his way to a small table against the wall, and settled down for the evening. As planned, Poundstack entered the rowdy dive at the appointed time, a place he wouldn't normally frequent on a dare, and took a seat on the opposite side of the room from Shlug. Sure enough, a few minutes later the bartender called out "Is there a Poundstack here?"

He had a pen ready, and two small bits of paper. At the phone he jotted down an address simple enough that he didn't need to duplicate it, and dropped it inconspicuously on Shlug's table as he made his exit, just in case there was an accomplice watching him.

On the scrap was written 'Main metro, under the clock', a place every Londoner knew. The big clock there was the largest in the country, second only to Big Ben.

The street was like a patchwork ribbon of varicolored drifting smoke that sparkled in tandem with the lights from the shop windows along the way. Poundstack went straight through the maze to his limousine, parked close by, and then, after waiting the agreed ten minutes, proceeded to the designated meeting place. Shlug, meanwhile, waited just five minutes before leaving the pub. He walked well out of sight of the place before attempting to hail a cab.

It wasn't that easy. Most of the passing cabs were occupied. But finally, out of the fog. Shlug spotted one with its 'available' light beaming, and managed to catch the driver's eye.

When they got to the big depot, throngs of citizens were milling about in a dizzying erratic jumble, the perfect place for brief encounters and quick exits. Shlug hurried inside to the big clock, where he very soon saw his boss nervously pacing back and forth.

The ransom collector had outsmarted himself. It would have been difficult to follow him if the transfer location had been a lonely pier on the docks or any other isolated place, but after Shlug saw the indistinctive man pass a large package to his employer, and his master pass an envelope in return, it was easy for him to follow the bloke out of the building, and along the busy street outside. Now the fog would be an advantage. It would slow the man's progress, no matter how near or far he'd be going, with much less chance of knowing he was being followed.

He wore a long brown coat, a hat and dark glasses. All standard apparel for his job. But dark glasses in the fog? He really couldn't be very bright. Oh, the glasses were gone when he turned around to be sure there was nobody closing behind him.

When he took a turn onto a side street, still on foot, Shlug quickly sought another cab, afraid he'd be spotted as the pedestrian traffic thinned out. It was easier to find one here, many of them circling the metro, watching for folks leaving the subway. He jumped in one of them and directed the driver into the same side street. Luckily, the one he pursued had to walk quite a bit further to reach his own car, so Shlug's cab easily slipped into place behind him as he pulled out into the slow motion traffic. "That buggar just pulled a ransom snatch on my buddy." Shlug told the driver in a calm voice that belied his excitement, "and I'm hoping to see where he goes."

"I'll do the best I can for you, lad" the driver assured him.

They dawdled along with the other cars through the muddy mist, both the driver and his passenger straining to keep one particular vehicle in sight.

Were they really following the right car? The right man? In this fog, there'd been several blind minutes, enough time for any plonker to step in the line-of-sight of the one you're after.

"I'll have a good tip for you if I can see where he stops without him seeing me," he entreated the driver.

Fortunately the car remained on a well-traveled boulevard, only turning onto a quiet street and driving one block before pulling off to park in a small open parking lot.

The cab cruised past and turned again before stopping in front of a large building completely out of sight of the car they'd been following. Shlug threw a five pound note into the front seat. What the hell... it was Poundstack's money.

"Good luck, mate," the cabbie said, and he seemed sincere.

"Wait for me." Shlug responded as he made a hasty exit from the car, and hurried back to the corner.

The mighty mite saw his man a good fifty yards ahead, and kept that distance between them until the rascal turned suddenly into a multi-storied building and disappeared. It was after business hours, but the front entrance was unlocked. Moving more cautiously now, Shlug soon ascertained there were more than a dozen business offices on three floors when he entered the lobby and saw the list of firms on a prominent billboard, along with their room numbers.

Had he come this far to lose him at the very end of the trail? It was late. Most of the offices were surely closed. There was nobody in sight on the main floor. It was as quiet as a midweek midnight in a mortuary, but a dim light coming through the front windows made it possible for him to make his way around without too much difficulty. Shlug made his way warily from door to door, listening for any sign of activity behind them. There didn't appear to be anybody conducting business or doing anything else on the premises. Total silence. He didn't use the elevator, it might be loud enough to be heard in a nearby office. He took the stairs to the second floor. Fortunately, his eyes had grown accustomed to the dark, and he could just make his way down the narrow corridor. He tiptoed from door to door. The third of the four doors on this floor had a logo and a name boldly engraved on it, which displayed for all to see: 'Continental Productions—Akbramin Moisting—President'.

Behind the door Shlug could hear a woman cackling and laughing, and a man's voice telling her to hush. He turned the doorknob slowly, quietly. It wasn't locked. He decided to make a dramatic entrance. Carefully he pushed the door open just far enough to clear the catch. Pulling out his club, which was big enough to look mortally dangerous when raised above his head, Shlug raised his right foot and kicked open the door with a loud crash!

"The jig's up, Moisting!" he cried out, waving the club and approaching them swiftly through the shadowed reception area with the frightful grimacing countenance of a madman. They were in the back room, the only room illuminated by an overhead light. He was counting the pile of bills on his desk, his frowzy moll standing beside him. Moisting blanched, his mouth agape, turning white in an instant, while Sasha Bugnam took frantic steps backward until she slammed into the far wall.

They were speechless, frozen in rigid paralysis, cowering in panic before the five foot four Shlug, who realized he could lower his club. In their eyes, he was ten feet tall, and could bite their heads off if he wanted to.

"Put the money back in the envelope." Shlug demanded, and Moisting wasted no time doing it. As he did, Shlug picked up a few of the man's calling cards, which sat in a little bowl on his desk.

"I'll let my employer know your name and address, in case he wants to contact you again. He doesn't like being robbed, so he might make a complaint to the police."

Moisting held out the envelope tentatively, desperately hoping this violent, unpredictable intruder would take it and depart.

Shlug grabbed it, slipped it into his shirt front, but had one more urgent question.

"What's your name, dolly?" he pointed directly at her, as if there were a few others in the room.

"Sasha," she whispered.

He jabbed his finger sharply and she thought she saw a laser bolt streaming from the tip.

"Sasha," she said in a loud voice, articulating clearly.

He jabbed again!

"Sasha Bugnum!" she almost screamed, which seemed to satisfy him.

Shlug backed toward the door, which hung precariously on one hinge, and left without another word.

It's amazing how fast panic can overwhelm people. Shlug had almost scared himself.

Chapter 67

Romance, long distance

CASEY, ABOUT READY TO TURN out the light and climb into bed, was startled when the phone rang. It was Robert. He'd been calling every quarter hour for quite a while, so he knew she was out, and wouldn't be asleep when he finally did get through.

"Have you given any more thought to coming back to New York," he inquired, trying to sound casual, as if it weren't of great importance to him.

"Yes, I did think about it, but I've decided to go back to London."

"Really?"

"It would just be putting off the inevitable if I went to New York. I don't know exactly how long I can stay in the states as a visitor, and even if I could stay for a year, I'd have to look for a job, and—"

He cut her off, "Sure, you've made a list of the obstacles, but have you also made a list of possibilities?"

"No, I haven't done that." she admitted, "but that list of obstacles is a big one."

"It's none of my business, but where were you earlier this evening?"

"Believe it or not, my father and I had dinner at Fred Astaire's place again."

Robert laughed. "He must be a lonely guy," was his immediate crack, but he hastened to say "not that you're not good company." which wasn't much of a save.

"I think he likes my father. He invited daddy Dingle to join him at a race track."

"Well, he's not a snob, that's for sure."

"Irving Berlin was there too, and an old actress named Vera Ellen. Have you ever heard of her?"

"Vera Ellen? Sure. She was very cute."

"She's quite shy. I always thought movie people were loud and arrogant, but Irving Berlin is shy too." She thought about it for a minute. "Actually, the only boisterous people at dinner tonight were my father and Fred Astaire's mother."

"And neither of them are show business people," Robert observed with a chuckle.

"It was nice of you to call," Casey figured they'd just about run out of conversation.

"It's your decision of course, but please change your mind and fly out this way for a few days," Robert implored, and somehow Casey got the impression it was important to him.

After they said goodbye, she slipped into bed and relaxed in the dark, rewinding the whole back and forth of their brief conversation. Most of it was shallow and impersonal, but she kept coming back to that one word near the end. Robert said 'please'.

Chapter 68

Jessie receives a proposal

"I've got something for you." he'd told her over the phone, so when Poundstack showed up with a big gift wrapped package tied with a bold red bow, Jessie opened it as fast as she could, trying not to look too eager, but expecting something like an ermine cape or a rare sculpture or something at least as grand. After all, it was her birthday, and her boyfriend was very rich.

So when she pulled out the reel of film he'd acquired with some difficulty from that scoundrel Moisting, it was a bit of a letdown. She tried not to let her disappointment show as he told her the details of how he and his loyal stable boy Shlug had secured her treasured print.

By the time he finished the details of the entire episode, they were seated comfortably on her couch, with drinks, nibbling on fresh baked cookies she'd prepared earlier that day as a present for herself.

It was wonderful of you to get this back for me, Mort," she purred affectionately, "It would be awful if it got out somehow, and Mr. Astaire found out about it."

"The only thing I can't figure out is how this chap Moisting got ahold of it in the first place."

"We might never know," she shrugged her shoulders as if it weren't of much concern to her how it had happened.

"I have something else for you," he grinned, which was a silly expression for a man of his age and usually serious deportment, "Happy birthday."

He pulled out an envelope and handed it to her.

"You did remember it was my birthday," she gushed.

"Well, my dear," he teased, "Your birthday is recorded in the public press. As a matter of fact, it was mentioned in a number of publications this week." He actually knew of only one industry magazine that dependably noted the birthdays of everyone in the entertainment world, a magazine Jessie subscribed to, but he wanted her to believe her birthday was important to everyone.

In the envelope was a first class ticket for a King-scaled month-long ocean cruise on the Queen Mary.

"I've got a ticket for myself, Jessie," he wanted to phrase his proposal just right, "and I'd like you to accompany me as my wife."

She didn't answer immediately, so he thrilled at the possibility she might have changed her mind at last.

"The ship stops at the Azores, Madeira and Canary Islands, Madrid, Lisbon and Cherbourg, on the coast of France. All exotic locales for a romantic getaway."

He was a charmer when he wanted to be, and Jessie had to phrase her answer just as charmingly, so he wouldn't be offended or so deflated that he wouldn't want to try again.

In the end, she did accompany him on the cruise, but it was as a single woman, so she could have a cabin to herself, and would be able to decide for herself just how much intimate time alone she cared to spend with Mr. Poundstack.

After two marriages and numerous affairs with initially fascinating men, all of whom tried to control and manipulate her, which led eventually to a complete breakdown and a lingering period of recuperation, Jessie was determined to chart her own course. If another relationship was in the cards, she was determined to be able to maintain at least equal footing.

As for the fresh print of her film, it was now available for private showings such as the one Robert Trabur had attended, but ironically, she never screened it again, and when an inventory of her effects was made years later upon her death, there was no mention of it.

Epilogue

How does it all turn out?

A FEW DAYS AFTER POUNDSTACK SAILED on the Queen Mary, the police were summoned to his residence, where the butler Cecil Cummings was found unconscious and badly wounded after receiving a severe blow to the head. He was hospitalized but able to attend the trial two months later of his attacker, after which he returned to his regular duties at the estate.

Max Goyings, wanted for the attempted murder of the butler Cecil Cummings, led the police on a high speed chase from the east of London, down the streets of Folkstone, all the way through the Eurotunnel. Driving his employer's high-powered Rolls Royce, Goyings endangered dozens of pedestrians and other vehicles on a harrowing high gear race through the city streets, stopping only upon reaching the quickly organized blockade in place at the Calais exit on the French side of the tunnel. He was tried, convicted and sentenced to five years in prison.

Commuted after two and a half years, he managed to secure employment driving a beer delivery lorry capable of a maximum forty miles per hour, which, shortly after, disappeared without a trace, along with the unrepentant felon, who was never seen again.

Akbramin Moisting, feeling frustrated and at a crossroads in his awkward personal journey through middle age, acting on a tip from a disreputable chum traveled to Australia, where, during that period, there was a paucity of soft porn materials. He stayed, and prospered, carving a new career for himself out of that far frontier of the British Empire.

Sasha Bugnam, deserted and desolate, left with a kiss and two weeks' severance pay, was so contrite and ashamed that she called Jessie and confessed all, including her last despicable act, lurking around her neighborhood for three days dressed as a suburban housewife, intercepting the mailman with a story convincing enough to persuade the fellow to put the package Robert had shipped from New York into her hands, rather than ringing Miss Matthews' bell, as he was supposed to do.

Jessie, reminded of her own often disreputable escapades as a teenager and beyond, in the hardscrabble back alleys of London and all over England before the Second World War, took Sasha under her wing, and did her best to put the lascivious lass on the straight and narrow path to a more proper future.

Asher Slinkring went on to appear in several of Kenneth Anger's short films, most often cast as Lucifer. Perceived as a spiritual figure by many, he eventually changed his name to Hareesh Jampheer, applied himself to the study of comparative religions, and after growing a full beard, wearing robes and sandals during his public appearances, enjoyed considerable success as a new age poet and philosopher.

The Arthur Treacher fish and chips chain turned out to be remarkably successful, with franchised restaurants in all but three of the United States. Treacher himself, thanks to his uncanny acumen in negotiating the original complicated contract, became quite wealthy in a few short years, eventually purchasing an estate of his own quite near the one in which he'd worked for Fred Astaire.

Dingle Thimble and Harleigh O'Halloran were hired by Fred Astaire to take Treacher's place. One favorable aspect of hiring them was the fact that both enjoyed playing the card game Flossie Austerlitz called cutthroat Pinocle. O'Halloran took care of most of the household duties, proving most able to assume a subservient attitude, and Dingle, in addition to serving as Astaire's chauffer, went along often with his employer as a personal tout to the various horse racing tracks in the state. It was Dingle, in fact, who introduced Astaire to a young female jockey named Robin.

During a break while taping the Dean Martin show, Martin confided to Gene Kelly that the Golddiggers, Martin's backup singers and foils during his comedy bits, would be headlining their own summer replacement hour, but they were short a couple of blonds to make up a full dozen. Naturally Kelly recommended the Goldcurls Twins, and Martin played a short nine holes of gold the day they were scheduled to audition, so he could be in attendance. Although a few years older than most of the others, Crystal and April fit right into the group, appeared as regulars for the full two seasons of the series, and were forever grateful to Gene Kelly for giving them their first bigtime opportunity in show business.

The parents of Debra Lavish finally received a letter from her a couple of years after her disappearance. She'd gone to Poland, figuring the novelty of being a natural blonde with blue eyes would be an advantage in securing roles in the burgeoning Polish film industry. She'd succeeded modestly, from her perspective at least, and impulsively married a fellow actor. Sadly, the wretch soon proved himself to be abusive and controlling.

Having discovered the hard way that divorce in a paternalistic country like Poland is almost an impossibility for a woman, unlike the maternalistic USA, where divorce and alimony is almost a sure thing even if based on the most trivial grounds, Debra begged her parents for money enough to bribe a judge. Well, not everyone's story has a happy ending.

Jay Leno never drove a cab again. He returned to the east coast and redoubled his efforts to establish a career as a stand-up comedian.

Robert Trabur's book of Lew Murgin's photos and backstage show biz anecdotes was quite successful, going into second printings in hardcover both in London as well as the United States. His career was further enhanced when he wrote a bestselling book about the fast evolving computer revolution, another of his many interests, and he ultimately became Algin Fingerroth's equal partner at Galactic Publishing Company.

Cassandra Thimble never returned to England after her marriage. She eventually established an exclusive riding academy a few miles south of Catskill State Park, in the state of New York, within commuting distance of Manhattan.

After giving birth to triplets, too busy now to handle both her business and her family, she implored her childhood friend Shlug Mugger to emigrate to America and take over the management of her riding academy, which he did.

Shlug and his wife Emily, the former Sasha Bugnum, who was now going by her given name in combination with Mugger, settled into their new home in the USA, and started a family of their own. The story of how Shlug and Sasha were reacquainted, fell in love and married, could fill a book. Suffice it to say that Sasha had finally found a man she could look up to.

Robert and Casey, having married on a whim to prevent her fast approaching scheduled flight back to London, and what was sure to be the oppressive supervision of her uncle, spent their honeymoon and several months in Debra's abandoned apartment to complete the terms of her lease, saving money to put up a down payment on their first house. It took many years for the pair to become a truly compatible and loving couple, but the process was aided by the positive attitude they both maintained during periods of stress, and the ever ascending quality of life they enjoyed as Robert's income and Casey's personal satisfaction improved in tandem.

Fred Astaire? Certainly everybody knows he lived a long and happy life, and his legacy of movie magic will endure forever.

And finally, concerning the naïve young boxer who sat on his hands while Bing Crosby was being accosted on that long ago day at Del Mar while the tiny jockey Willy Shoemaker jumped up to take charge: After winning a gold medal at the Olympics, the promising pugilist turned pro, changed his name from Cassius Clay to Muhammad Ali, and eventually became the undisputed heavyweight boxing champion of the entire world.

THE END